JONATHAN LATIMER

RED GARDENIAS

NO EXIT PRESS

1989

No Exit Press
18 Coleswood Road
Harpenden, Herts AL5 1EQ

British Library Cataloguing in Publication Data

Latimer, Jonathan 1906–1983
    Red Gardenias – (No Exit Press Vintage Crime)
    I. Title
813′.52[F]

ISBN 0 948353 40 6

9 8 7 6 5 4 3 2 1

Printed by William Collins, Glasgow

To
HUGH KAHLER

CHAPTER I

"THERE'S A BURGLAR downstairs," Ann Fortune said.

"A burglar?" William Crane sat up in the colonial four-poster, blinked his eyes in the light. "A burglar?"

"He didn't send up a card," Ann said.

Crane modestly pulled the patchwork quilt about him. "Let him burgle." Ash-gray, like cigarette smoke, his breath hung in the air. "It isn't our house."

"Everyone thinks it is."

"Do we care what a burglar thinks?"

"Yes." She tried not to smile, but her sea-green eyes crinkled at the corners. "You have to go down and shoot him."

"Oh, very well," he said. "I'll go down and shoot him in the leg."

He swung his feet over the side of the bed. The air was very cold near the floor. He put his feet back under the covers.

She watched from the bedroom door. "Well?"

"You're beautiful," he said.

"Aren't you going to shoot him?"

"Beautiful, blonde . . . and bloodthirsty!"

"Not so loud. You'll frighten him."

"I hope I do."

"You're a fine, brave detective. I thought——" She hesitated for a halved second. "Hear him?"

There was a tinkling noise downstairs. A breath of November wind, rustling the shades, momentarily silenced it; then, in a lull, they heard it again. Crane was favorably impressed.

"I think he's pouring a drink."

"He's in the living room," Ann said.

"He could pour a drink in the living room, couldn't he?"

A Nile-green robe, drawn close, revealed her slender figure. "Bill!" Her hair was as pale as Manila rope. "As head of this household, it's your duty . . . "

"All right," he said hastily. "But I'm inexperienced with burglars."

"Now's your chance to learn."

"What a wife you'll make some guy." He shuddered as his feet touched the floor. "It's cold, too."

"In the eyes of the world, I *am* your wife."

"Not in the eyes of God . . . yet."

"And never," she said. "Hurry up."

"I think he's gone."

"No."

He put on slippers and a Scotch-plaid dressing gown. He took a police .38 out of a pigskin zipper bag. "If I'm killed you'll have me on your conscience."

She said, "It won't be much of a load."

He went by her at the door, thinking how nice it would be to kiss her. He liked her skin, stained the color of cornhusks by the sun, and the way her green eyes crinkled at the corners. He almost wished he was married to her.

"Good-by now," she said.

Halfway down the stairs he thought he might have pretended he was really saying good-by to her and so kissed her. He almost went back to attempt this, but he didn't. He remembered he was stalking a burglar. That was a serious business.

By leaning over the banister he could see a sliver of banana-colored light near the living-room door. He would have liked to fire a couple of shots down the stairs and frighten the burglar away, but he supposed he had to capture him. He and Ann had just been assigned to what might be a murder case by their agency, and it was possible the burglar was connected with it in some way.

Besides, it was a rented house and the shots wouldn't be good for the rugs.

He crept down a few steps and discovered he was a little frightened. He wondered if he ought to rush in and overpower the man, or simply shoot him. He remembered with growing indignation the calm manner in which Ann had sent him downstairs. Women were queer. They'd fuss over a man going out in a rainstorm or on a fishing trip, but they'd send him after a burglar as offhandedly as they would for the morning milk.

He crossed the hall and peeped in the living room. Dim rays from a parchment-shaded desk lamp made a half circle of blue and oyster white on an Aubusson rug, lost themselves in shadows on high blue walls, reappeared like fireflies in a crystal chandelier. Over the desk, over bright sheets of paper, a man leaned. As Crane watched, he tore one of the papers, let the pieces flutter into a metal wastebasket. He took a drink from a glass by the lamp.

Crane thought it was a damn funny way for a burglar to act. He reached into the room and snapped on the overhead lights. "Put your hands up," he ordered.

Getting to his feet, the man knocked over his glass. "What the deuce!" Two ice cubes fell on the blue-and-white Aubusson.

"That's what I say," said Crane.

He was a young, good-looking burglar. He had very black hair and heavy, straight eyebrows and he wore a tweed suit. It was a well-tailored suit; gray with flecks of green and red in it.

"I'm unarmed," he said. "You can put your gun away."

"It's all right," Crane assured him. "I'm not sure it's loaded."

"You're Mr Crane?"

Crane nodded and said, "You have the advantage of me."

The young man stared pointedly at Crane's revolver. "I'd hardly say that."

"Possibly not," Crane agreed. He looked at the litter of papers on the desk. There were letters, some bills, some typewritten documents. He looked at the overturned glass. "Do you carry a flask?" he asked.

"Didn't Dad show you the liquor?" the young man said.

"Does your father burgle, too?"

"Maybe I ought to explain," said the young man. "My father is Simeon March."

"Oh!" Crane toed the ice cubes on the Aubusson.

"We didn't expect you until tomorrow," the young man said.

"We flew," Crane said. "Your father . . . if he is your father . . . wasn't home, but the butler brought us over." He frowned, thinking hard. "But that doesn't explain . . ."

"I know." The young man moved toward a white damask chair. "Mind if I sit down?"

"Do you mind if I do, too?"

A smile erased sullen lines at the corners of young March's mouth, made his face pleasant. He sat on the damask chair. Crane selected a sofa covered with soft blue velvet. He thought the room must have been furnished by an interior decorator, so carefully blended were the blues and whites.

Young March said conversationally, "This house belonged to my cousin, Richard March."

"So I was told."

Crane thought the decorations had been selected to match the Aubusson. There were on the windows white taffeta curtains, drawn close at their middles with a blue cord so that each curtain looked like half of a very graceful woman wearing a Grecian robe. Over the white marble fireplace was a blue-framed mirror. Lilies, on an eighteenth-century English mahogany table, arched their necks above a crystal vase.

"I wanted to clean out Richard's correspondence,"

the young man said. "He had a number of feminine friends——" As black, as straight as penny licorice sticks, his eyebrows nearly met over his nose. "You know—there might be something compromising—a note or something."

"To Richard or the ladies?"

"Oh, Richard." His eyes were on the ice cubes. "You know—the family name." The water made dark circles on the rug.

"You didn't think the name would be safe with me?"

"I didn't know."

The sofa gave under Crane's neck. "Well, that's all right." A spring pinged in the sofa. "But you might have rung the bell."

"As I said, I didn't know you were here."

"That's so." Crane pushed against the sofa, let the rebound help him to his feet. "I guess it's all right." He waved at the papers. "Take 'em. But one thing . . . a favor?"

"Sure."

"Where did you get that drink?"

The white-enameled butler's pantry proved to have a liquor cabinet. Crane selected a bottle of scotch, asked, "Have one with me?" March nodded and they took glasses and the bottle back to the living room. Ann Fortune was there.

"I thought maybe the burglar had killed you," she said.

Crane knew this was a lie because she had put on lipstick. The Nile-green robe went well with her rope-colored hair. He said, "This is our burglar, Ann."

Ann smiled. "It looks as though you'd joined the union."

"No," said March. "He's a very efficient house-holder. My name is Peter March. Will you have a drink?"

"I think that would be nice."

"Here, darling." Crane gave her his glass, said, "Mr March is the son of Simeon March."

Her brows arched over green eyes. "With all those millions behind him, does he have to housebreak?"

Peter March laughed boyishly. Crane said, "He didn't expect us until tomorrow."

"We didn't expect him, either." She sat on the blue sofa, drew her knees under her. "It was polite of him to call, though." Her slim legs were tan.

"Now, really," Peter March objected with a smile. "I can explain everything."

"He has," said Crane.

"Everything's all right?" Ann asked.

"Certainly."

"Then why don't you put that gun away, darling?"

Crane was astonished to find the revolver in his hand. He put it on the desk, beside the pile of papers. Peter March said, "I was hoping someone would think of that."

Crane put two fingers of whisky in a glass. "Here's to bigger burglaries."

They all drank. Ann covered her ankles with a fat pillow. "Is it always as cold as this in November?"

"It gets pretty cold, but we like it," March said. "It brings the ducks down."

"I love duck," Ann said.

"Do you? If he likes, I'll take your husband out to our duck club."

Crane said, "I'm not such a shot."

"That's all right."

"I'd like to, then."

"Fine. Next Sunday."

Ann asked what wives did while their husbands shot duck.

"It depends upon the kind of wives they are," Peter March said.

Crane said, "She's the worst kind." He grinned at Ann.

"Then she'll have a cocktail party. That's the custom

of Marchton's upper-crust wives." Against March's dark skin, his teeth looked very white. "They pretend they drink in protest."

Crane said, "She'll stay home and sew while I'm away."

"I'll sew nothing," Ann said, "unless it's wild oats."

Crane saw admiration in Peter March's eyes. He didn't blame him. Maybe he shouldn't have objected so strenuously to working with Ann. But she was the boss's niece—that was bad. He hadn't wanted a relative of the boss to see how he handled a case. He supposed he would hardly dare take a drink while she was around.

Peter March told them his father had arranged for them to become members of the Country and City clubs.

"That's decent of him," Crane said.

"And this house is lovely," Ann added.

"Dick's wife, Alice, just finished decorating it before they got divorced," Peter March said, his face not quite so pleasant. "She had a man—at least he wore trousers —all the way from New York to do the work." His eyebrows were back in two absolutely straight lines. "It cost Dick close to twenty thousand."

He sounded as though he didn't approve of the expenditure. Crane wondered what had happened to Richard. He thought maybe he was dead.

"It was terribly nice of you to let us have it," Ann said.

Peter March put down his glass, offered her a cigarette. She took one and he lit a match. "Dad was glad to get it rented," he said. "It belongs to the estate." He lit his own cigarette. "It's for sale . . . no bids."

Crane said, "It is a swell layout. All we had to do was hang up our hats."

"We were pleased to fix it up. It isn't often we can pick up as good an advertising man. Our advertising department needs some life." Peter March raised his glass, held it to his lips, spoke over it. "I've been after Dad a year to get somebody good."

"Sometimes I'm pretty bad," Crane said.

Ann said, "Dear, you're a wonderful copy writer."

Crane scowled at her, drawing his brows down toward his nose, but this apparently had no effect.

"He has what is known as F. A.," she explained to Peter March. "Feminine appeal."

Crane had to laugh. He said, "I'm known as Casanova Crane, the Copy-Writing Cad."

"You're good if you can put sex appeal in a washing machine," Peter March said.

He was smiling again, and Crane noticed the difference it made in his appearance. In his age, too. In repose his face looked sullen, mostly because of his utterly straight brows and the downcurve of his lips. It looked middle aged. Smiling, he was boyish, almost handsome. Crane supposed he was about twenty-eight.

"Will you have another drink?" he asked.

Peter March said he'd have a small one. They all had a small one. Then March looked at his wrist watch. "I've got to go." He shook Ann's hand; an unnecessary gesture, Crane thought. "This is the nicest burglary I've ever committed," he told her.

"Please break in again," Ann said.

Crane said, "Our front door is always locked to you."

"Thank you." March was half a head taller than Ann. He was smiling again. "If you haven't a car we've plenty. You may want to look the town over tomorrow."

"Why, that's nice . . . " Ann began, smiling up at him.

Crane broke in, "We've got one on the way from New York. Williams, our general factotum, is driving it with our belongings."

Peter March said, "But if he doesn't get here——"

"We'll be glad to use yours," Ann said.

March moved toward the table with the parchment-shaded lamp. "I'll get my papers and——"

A hollow, metallic voice from the door said, "No, buddy. No, you won't. Keep your mitts off that desk."

A thin man in a blue overcoat stood by the living-room door. Crane had an idea he had been there for a considerable time. A white handkerchief masked the lower part of his face; a felt hat shadowed his eyes. He had an automatic pistol.

"I'll take them papers," he said.

Crane had never heard a voice like the man's. It had a resonance, as though he was talking through a piece of gas pipe. It sounded as though he had a tin larynx. His breath made a whistling noise, too, when he spoke.

"Get over with them others," he said to Peter March.

Crane said, "This house is about as private as the Grand Central Station."

"Don't get wise," the man whispered. "I don't want to sap anybody, see?" A button was missing off the left sleeve of his overcoat.

Waving Peter March aside with the pistol, he advanced on the table. Ann Fortune watched him through cucumber-green eyes. He put a handful of papers in his overcoat pocket.

"No," said Peter March. "You can't do that."

He started for the man, and for an instant Crane was certain he was about to be shot. The man looked frightened, undecided. Crane held his breath. Then the man hit March on the temple with the barrel of his pistol.

Crane saw his wrist was small. The bone was a blue-white, like the wristbone of a man who has been begging in winter. March fell down, but he wasn't badly hurt. Ann started to scream.

"Now, sister . . . " the man whispered.

Ann was silent. The man put the rest of the papers in his overcoat pocket. He saw the revolver, put that in his pocket. He pointed his pistol at Crane.

"That all?"

"That's all I know about," Crane said.

"What about you, March?"

March sat on the Aubusson, both hands pressed to his temple. "I don't know anything about them," he said sullenly.

"Like hell!" The man's voice, with that metallic quality, sounded Chinese. "I heard you tell our friends why you was here."

"All right," March said.

"Yeah, but it ain't." The man stood over March, but his eyes, the pistol were on Crane. "A certain party don't want anybody nosin' around."

"All right," March said.

The man took two quick steps, reached a hand in March's inside coat pocket, pulled out three letters, all the time keeping the pistol pointed at Crane.

He jeered, "So you don't know nothin', Mister March?"

"Listen," March began. "I'll give . . ."

"Stow it." The man raised the pistol as though he was going to backhand March's face. "They'll be safe where they're going." He bent his body so that his face was near March's. "Safe, see?"

"Where are they going?" Crane asked.

"Keep your nickel outa this, wise guy," the man said, going to the door.

Ann asked, "Isn't he going to take our money?"

"Don't give him ideas," Crane said.

The man paused at the hall entrance. "Lady, you got me all wrong." It was hard to hear what he was saying. "I'm here on business."

"Oh," Ann said.

"I ain't a heister, see?"

"I see," Ann said. She didn't.

"O.K., lady."

The man went out into the hall, and presently they heard the front door slam. Peter March got to his feet. An automobile engine roared about half a block away; the automobile went off very fast in second gear.

"Are you all right?" Ann asked Peter March.

He took his hands from his temple. There was no

blood, only the swollen place where he had been hit. "Damn him," he said. "Who could have sent him?"

Ann asked, "Were the letters very important?"

"To the March family. Maybe to some of Richard March's women, too."

"Richard must be fascinating," Ann said.

Peter March's face was grim. "A lot of women thought so."

Crane found his glass, was pleasantly surprised to find whisky in it. "You told me you were destroying the incriminating items," he said. He drank the whisky.

March nodded.

"But the letters in your pocket . . .?"

"Oh, those?" March took his time answering. "I was . . . going to destroy those at home."

Ann said, "I think I hear the doorbell."

They listened. A bell was tinkling persistently somewhere in the house.

Crane said, "I hope it's not the postman—with more letters."

CHAPTER II

UNDER THE WHITE porch light was a woman in a magnificently marked mink coat. She was a slender woman and her hair glistened darkly. Back of her, obscured by shadow, stood a man.

"Is this Mr Crane?" she inquired.

"Carmel!" Peter March moved past Crane, held the door open. "And Dad! What are you doing here?"

Simeon March followed the woman into the house, walking with hard, abrupt steps. He was the richest man in his state; owner of March & Company, the nation's second largest manufacturer of electric washing machines and refrigerators; founder of Marchton, and chairman of the March Foundation for Medical Research.

For Crane, he had another distinction. He was, for the moment, his employer.

In the blue-and-white living room Peter March made the proper introductions. The dark woman's name was Carmel March. Looking at Simeon March, Crane wondered who Carmel March was. Not Richard March's wife; her name was Alice. He put this problem away to answer Simeon March's questions.

"At the last minute we came by airplane," he said. "That's why we're early."

Simeon March had perfectly white hair, heavy pepper-and-salt eyebrows, a drooping mustache, and brown eyes the color of maple sugar. The skin on his face and hands was discolored; it was mostly tan, but there were dark brown patches. He was very wrinkled, almost like an old Indian. He made Crane think of Theodore Roosevelt without in the least looking like him.

He started to say something else to Crane, but an exclamation from Carmel halted him.

"Peter! What's the matter?" She came across the room to him, her dark eyes on the bruise over his temple. "How did you hurt yourself?"

"It isn't anything," Peter said.

"But it is." Her voice was anxious; she turned to Crane. "How did it happen?"

Crane told her, thinking as he talked she was very beautiful. There was a masklike quality about her oval face, but her anxiety over Peter March gave it, for the moment, a lovely mobility. She was one of the most

vividly colored women he had ever seen—India-ink
hair, raspberry lips, milk-of-magnesia skin, and eyes . . .
eyes so dark, so luminous, so liquid they made him
think of very strong coffee.

"But why the devil did you try to stop him?" Simeon
March gruffly asked his son when Crane finished.

"He could use the letters for blackmail," Peter said.

Simeon March grunted. "Let him try."

"He got all of them, Peter?" Carmel asked. "*All* of
them?"

"Yes."

She had forgotten about his bruise. She sat on the
sofa, let the mink fall away from her, revealing exquisite
shoulders. "That's strange," she said softly. She wore a
black evening gown of tulle, cut so low in front it exposed a blue-shadowed hollow between her breasts.

Crane caught Ann's eyes, green and narrow, on him
and he grinned. Let her admire Peter March; he had
something to admire, too. He wondered again who
Carmel was; she seemed pretty exotic to be a March,
except by marriage.

Peter was explaining it to his father that he had
wanted to destroy Richard's personal documents before
the house was occupied. "I just thought of it," he said.

Simeon March demanded, "Did you call the police?"

"If you call the police there 'll be publicity," Peter warned.

Crane said, "The man spoke of getting the papers for someone."

"It sounded like blackmail," Peter said.

"Blackmail a dead man?" Simeon March grunted. "Huh!"

Crane thought with considerable pride that he had guessed correctly about Richard. He wondered how long he had been dead.

"This sounds like a mystery drama," Ann said.

"Doesn't it, though?" Carmel March said.

Simeon March stared at her. "You could have prevented this," he growled. "You had a whole year to destroy Richard's papers."

Carmel asked, "Why should I have thought to destroy them?" Her voice was brittle.

For a moment her eyes met his in a defiant stare, then Simeon March swung around to his son, "*You* could have done it."

"I should have," Peter admitted. "But I never thought until today."

Simeon March's anger made his eyes topaz yellow. "Stupid," he snarled.

Crane thought he'd hate to cross the millionaire. He

wasn't the kind of man you'd try any slick business tricks on. To avert a further explosion, he said, "Will anyone have a drink?"

"I will," Ann said. "I always will."

The others accepted, too. Carmel offered to help get ice and glasses, but Ann refused.

"Sooner or later I'm going to have to explore that kitchen," she said. "It might as well be now."

"I'll go along as a bodyguard," Crane said.

Glistening with porcelain and chromium, the kitchen looked as fancy as the ones in magazine advertisements. There was a double sink, an electric stove, an electric dishwasher, and the largest refrigerator Crane had ever seen. He opened the refrigerator door gingerly.

"What's the matter?" Ann asked.

"I was afraid a corpse would come tumbling out."

"Richard's?" Ann asked.

"Someone's," Crane said. "It's a poor case where they haven't got a corpse tucked around the house."

Ann found a tray and high glasses in the pantry. "I think it's a nice case."

"You would." Crane jerked out a rubber ice tray, squeezed cubes of ice into one of the sinks. "I saw you giving Peter March the gladeye."

She said, "You were rubbering at Carmel, too."

He found some seltzer and they went into the living room. After everyone had a drink Simeon March said:

"Crane, I'd like to have a word with you."

"Dad, no business now," Peter said. "This is the middle of the night."

"We'll only be a moment," Simeon March said.

Crane followed him into the library, sat down beside him on a leather davenport. "D'you know why you're here?" Simeon March asked him.

All four walls of the library, except where there were narrow windows and a high fireplace, were lined with books. Most of them were bound in leather with illuminated titles, largely in gold; and they ran in matched sets. Crane decided they had been bought for appearance, rather than reading.

"I've got a rough idea," he said.

"Then I won't have to tell you . . ."

Crane interrupted him. "I wish you would." He hadn't the least idea what the case was about, but he thought he ought to bluff. "I'd like to get the straight story."

"All right." Jerkily, Simeon March produced two cigars. Crane started to duck, so violent was the motion. "Have one?" asked Simeon March.

"No, thanks."

"Don't smoke?"

"Yes. Cigarettes."

"A woman's smoke."

This satisfactorily settled, Simeon March told his story. As he went along Crane felt a thrill of excitement. The case, if facts bore out the old man's inferences, looked like a humdinger.

Nine months ago, in February, Richard March had been discovered dead at the steering wheel of his sedan beside the Country Club at the conclusion of the dance. A defective heater had been blamed for his death by a coroner's jury.

"Your son?" Crane asked.

"My late brother's son. Joseph March's son."

Crane thought Mr March sounded as though he expected him to know who Joseph was, so he nodded as if he did know.

"Was there a defective heater?" he asked.

A look of grim humor came into Simeon March's wrinkled face. "I don't know. Nobody inquired."

"But why not?"

"People accepted his removal gratefully, without inquiring into whys and wherefores."

"He wasn't popular?"

"He was a complete wastrel."

"Didn't he work for March & Company?"

"Yes and no." Simeon March discovered the cigar was out. "Damn this thing!" He violently struck a match. "Richard was general manager in charge of sales." Air made a sucking noise through the cigar. "But I never heard of his working."

Crane nodded. "And then——"

Simeon March took a long pull at the cigar, blew the smoke out hard. "And then my John died."

He told of his death without evidence of emotion, but the hand holding the burning match trembled. He didn't look at Crane while he talked.

John had died just a month ago. He had apparently been trying to fix his motor in his garage ("He was a first-rate mechanic," Simeon March interpolated.) and had been overcome by carbon monoxide. His body was on the floor. The hood over the engine was up and there were tools on the car's running board. Carmel March had discovered him.

"His wife?" Crane asked.

"Yes."

Crane reflected that Carmel seemed pretty cheerful for a widow of a month's standing. She was wearing black, but her attitude . . .

He broke this train of thought to ask: "How did the doors happen to be closed? A mechanic should have known——"

"There was a strong wind that day. Supposed to have blown the doors shut."

"Two carbon-monoxide deaths." Crane frowned. "Quite a coincidence. What was the coroner's verdict?"

"Like the other—accidental."

"Well, there are a lot of accidental deaths that way . . . and a lot of suicides."

"John wouldn't kill himself."

"What about Richard?"

"Richard was drunk when he died." Simeon March's voice showed his dislike for Richard. "You don't kill yourself when you're drunk."

"I never have," Crane admitted. He scratched the back of his neck. "Do you have any proofs of murder?"

"Do you think I would have hired you if I had?"

"But your suspicions were aroused by something?"

"Yes."

"By what?"

Simeon March stood up. His jaw was set. "I'd rather not say." He chewed his cigar. "I want you to make an independent investigation. If you find anything, come to any conclusion, I want to know about it. That's all."

"All right." Crane stood up, too. "Does anyone know Miss Fortune and I are detectives?"

"No one."

"Not even your son, Peter?"

"Not even Peter. And nobody must know, you understand? That's why I've had you pose as an employee of the advertising department. I want you to mingle with John's friends without arousing suspicion."

"It's a good setup," Crane said. "Provided I can write advertisements for washing machines."

"If you get in trouble I can arrange for a New York agency to write them for you."

"Maybe I'll turn out all right," Crane said.

"The only thing I don't like about the scheme is the agency's idea of your pretending to be married."

"Colonel Black thought a married couple would mix more easily."

"But aren't you likely to compromise Miss Fortune?"

"It's like taking a secretary on a business trip," Crane said. "Nobody thinks anything of that now."

"Well, it's her problem." Simeon March chewed his cigar. "When will you have something for me?"

Crane raised his shoulders. "It's a pretty large order. Especially when there's such a lapse of time."

"Do as much as you can."

Crane said, "I'll keep . . . "

Carmel March entered the room, smiled at Crane, said, "He's a slave driver, isn't he?" Then, to Simeon March, "Dad, I'll run along with Peter."

"All right."

She smiled again at Crane. "Good night."

"Good night."

She was taller than Crane had thought, and she walked with long, graceful steps. She had a beautiful figure. He watched her until she went out the door. She smelled of gardenias.

"How long had John been married?" he asked Simeon March.

"Six years."

"Any children?"

"No." Simeon March's face was expressionless. "None."

Crane thought he caught a note deeper than irony in Simeon March's tone. He debated about his next question for an instant, then decided to ask it. Certainly, the trend of the conversation invited it.

"Did they get along well?" he inquired.

Simeon March shook his head. "No." He walked to one of the windows overlooking the driveway. "John was a serious boy. He was a worker. . . ." His voice died away.

"And Carmel?"

"She didn't help him. She liked to go out. Parties, dancing . . ."

Crane walked to the window, stood just in back of March. "And when John wouldn't take her out she went out anyway?"

The old man didn't answer.

Crane asked, "Is there a motive which would link the deaths, Mr March?"

"I can't say."

"Can't or won't?"

Simeon March was silent.

There were voices in the drive. Peter March was helping Carmel into a green convertible with white-wall tires. She was laughing and they heard her say, "You're going to have a swell shiner tomorrow, Peter. I know the signs."

"I'll say you gave it to me," Peter said. "I'll tell everybody you got tight and let me have it."

Crane said to Simeon March, "You must have had a reason for hiring detectives. You must suspect someone."

"I do."

"Who?"

Simeon March shook his head. "I told you I'd rather not say. I don't——"

Carmel March's voice was very distinct. "Let's do go and get tight, Peter," she called.

Peter went around the car. "All right." He got in and backed down the driveway. They were laughing about something. The car disappeared behind a row of elms.

"John . . . now Peter!" Simeon March stared at the empty driveway, suddenly wheeled on Crane. "There's your murderer! Tie a rope around her neck, Detective. Stand her on the gallows." His voice was hoarse, almost indistinct. "I'll see the trap is sprung."

CHAPTER III

BREAKFAST WAS SERVED by a large colored lady who arrived at seven-thirty and said her name was Beulah. She brought with her a young colored girl to assist in the housework.

Crane felt pretty well. He hadn't had enough sleep because he had spent an hour before going back to bed telling Ann Fortune of the deaths from carbon monoxide and of Simeon March's accusation of Carmel, but then he hardly ever had enough sleep. Between the cereal and the eggs, he tried to piece together the scraps of paper thrown by Peter March in the living-room wastebasket. Ann came to the table.

"Any luck?"

She was, he had to admit, a nice example of what nature could do in the way of a blonde. She was wearing a pair of blue lounging pajamas which contrasted very well with her tanned skin and her eyes, turquoise this morning.

"Not much." He grinned at her. "Aren't you going to kiss me good morning?"

It appeared that she wasn't. She sat across the table from him, pulled some of the scraps to her. Deftly, she pieced together two liquor bills. They were for June and July and showed by their size that Richard March had entertained extensively.

Crane assembled one more, and then Ann found a more interesting note; written on half a sheet of fine linen paper in purple ink. It was dated July 15, and read:

DARLING,

Can't make Brookfield this W. E. Business. Stop Dairy.

DELIA

Crane was interested. "That sounds as though Richard was up to something immoral."

The second letter, also in violet ink, read:

S. is sprung. He's heard something, so be careful if you can't be good. I hope you can't.

DELIA

"Ah!" Crane drunk the last of his coffee. "Trouble looms."

Ann said, "It's awfully ominous. Bill, what does 'sprung' mean?"

"Freed from a bastille."

"Oh!" She looked to see if he was serious, then asked, "What's a heister? I ought to know words like those, hadn't I, if I'm to catch criminals?"

He told her a heister was a stick-up man.

"S. sounds nasty," Ann said. "Going around hearing things."

"He probably wouldn't overlook a week end."

"Not with a passionate woman like Delia."

Crane spoke to her severely. "How can you tell Delia is passionate? I think she's very reserved, just signing her name to the letters."

"The violet ink," Ann said. "You don't write business letters in violet ink."

"It depends upon what business you're in," Crane said.

Beulah brought more coffee. "Is everything all right, ma'am?" she asked Ann.

"It's fine, Beulah."

Crane leaned back in his chair, sighed mournfully. "I suppose I'd better report to March & Company."

"Aren't you going to do anything about Delia?"

"I'll see if I can hear of somebody named Delia."

"I'll find her," Ann said.

"If somebody named Delia calls on you, you will."

"No, I'll find her."

"Am I supposed to keep house while you're doing this?"

"No. I'll just find her. There's no reason why I can't detect."

"No reason except blondes don't have brains."

"You'll see."

"O.K.," Crane said. "But I bet I get her first."

"Champagne?"

"Sure."

"It's a bet."

They shook hands. Ann's hand felt smooth and slender. Crane asked, "What are you going to do?"

"Do you think I'd give away the secrets of my profession?"

"Gosh!" He was impressed. "You're beginning to talk like a detective."

"I am a detective," Ann said. "Just because you didn't want me to come along doesn't mean——"

"You were the boss's niece."

"You were afraid I would tell him how much you drank?"

"No," Crane lied. "The thing was I hadn't seen you in blue pajamas."

Ann looked as though she might blush, and said, "About the deaths, what do you want me to find out from Carmel?" She didn't look angry. "She's coming over this morning."

"Maybe I won't go to work," Crane said.

"You'll go to work if I have to send for the police," Ann declared. "What do you want me to find out?"

"I don't know." He looked at his coffee cup, but it was empty. "What 'd you and Carmel talk about while I was with old man March?"

"Just ordinary small talk." Ann tinkled the bell on the table. "How stuffy a small town is . . . the best shops . . . where to get your hair done . . . places to go at night . . . "

Crane asked eagerly, "Did you get the names of some good joints?"

Beulah came in and said, "Yes, ma'am?" Ann said, "More coffee for Mr Crane." Pleased, Crane thought it might be nice to have a thoughtful girl like Ann around the house. Particularly one as seductive in a pair of pajamas. He wondered if she had slept with her bedroom door locked.

Ann continued, "They both seemed awfully nervous."

Crane said, "They seemed pretty interested in each other, too."

"Do you think so?" she asked coldly, as if she didn't like the idea.

"When a dame almost weeps over a guy's wound I wonder." Crane put sugar in his coffee. "You notice, she didn't worry whether I had a wound or not."

"Give her time."

Crane laughed, then said, "Carmel scares me. Especially after hearing old man March accuse her. I'd hate to have her pump me full of carbon monoxide."

Ann said, "Bill, do you *really* think those people were murdered?"

"Carmel 'd have a good motive."

Ann's green eyes were thoughtful. "She'd certainly have some money if she blotted out the entire March family."

"Twenty millions or so."

"A girl could dress well on that."

It had turned out to be a fine morning. Sunlight the color of overripe Camembert cheese flooded the cement driveway, made the lawn a bright green. Two businesslike robins looked for bugs in the grass.

Ann said, "Of course, Peter has the same motive as Carmel."

"Sure. If he lives he gets the dough."

"But I'm sure he didn't do it," Ann said.

"Why?"

"Well . . . he doesn't look like a murderer."

Crane groaned. "And you claim to be a detective!"

"I'm sorry," Ann said, and added, "but if he's a suspect he's your suspect."

"No. My suspect is Carmel."

"They're your suspects. I give them to you."

"All right," Crane said. "But what's left for you?"

"Oh, I'll dig up something."

"Don't get a secondhand suspect," Crane warned her. "They're not reliable."

"If I want I can have the bandit."

"You can if he isn't a friend of Peter."

"How could he be a friend of Peter? He hit him in the face, didn't he?"

"I know," Crane said. "But do you think Peter would have gone after him unless he was sure the man wouldn't shoot?" He put out his cigarette. "You didn't see me going after the man, did you?"

"No, I didn't."

"You don't have to be nasty about it."

"I wasn't. I just said, 'No, I didn't!'"

"I wouldn't be surprised," Crane said, "if the man came to help Peter, to act as a lookout."

"No," Ann said. "The bandit called him March. Don't you remember?"

"Sure, but . . ."

"He wouldn't have called him by name if he was an accomplice. His idea would have been to pretend he didn't know him."

"Maybe blondes have brains at that."

Ann said, "You see who'll drink the champagne."

"I will," Crane said stoutly.

The doorbell rang and Beulah brought in Peter March.

"Beulah," he asked, "you fix the Cranes a good breakfast?"

"Yes, Mister Peter," Beulah giggled.

"Beulah used to work for Richard. She knows the house," Peter explained. "That's why Dad had her come."

"We found her this morning on our doorstep," Crane said. "We thought she was a waif."

"How's your wound?" Ann inquired.

"It's fine," Peter said.

"You were pretty brave."

"I wasn't really." Peter March looked down at her. "I just got mad at the thought of losing those letters."

To Crane's critical eye he didn't look as though he'd gone on much of a bender with Carmel. His face was clean shaven, and there was a touch of color in his cheeks. His straight black brows, in daylight, didn't seem so heavy. A smile made his face pleasant.

"Have you heard from the guy?" Crane asked.

March looked at him sharply. "Why should I have?"

Crane's face was innocent. "Didn't you say something about blackmail last night?"

"That was just excitement." Peter March's face relaxed. "I don't think there was anything really dangerous in those letters."

Crane wanted to ask him, then, why the bandit was so eager to get them, but he decided he'd better not appear too interested.

"I hope the guy doesn't come back," he said.

Peter March smiled at Ann. "You're not afraid, are you?" He was really quite good looking when he smiled.

"Certainly I am," Ann said.

He stared at her admiringly. "You didn't look scared last night."

Crane thought, what the hell! Was this competition? The rich man's son and the poor employee's wife. Of course, Ann wasn't really his wife, but he suddenly decided he did not like Peter.

"I was scared, though," Ann said.

Peter said, "I won't believe it." He was looking into

her green eyes. "But I'm sure there won't be any more armed men." He turned to Crane. "Like a ride to the office?"

Ann's voice was silky. "Bill 'd love it. It's terribly nice of you to think of stopping for him."

What the hell! Crane thought again. He was damned glad he was not really married. He said, "I'll get a hat and coat." He thought of something. "And I'll have to kiss the little woman good-by."

He hoped "little woman" would make her mad. He knew the kiss would. He got his hat and a camel's-hair topcoat and bent over her. He saw Peter March watching. He determined to make as much of the kiss as possible. She had to endure it; she was posing as his wife.

"Good-by now, darling," he said.

It wasn't quite the triumph he thought it would be. He kissed her with gusto. She bit his lip with even more gusto.

CHAPTER IV

ON HIS FINE mahogany desk the black-and-silver clock read ten past three when William Crane pushed the button for Miss Kirby. She was his secretary. She entered his office and waited in front of his desk, notebook in hand.

"Miss Kirby, I suffer from visions," Crane said.

An alarmed expression came upon Miss Kirby's thin face. "Yes sir," she said dubiously. She was a pale, middle-aged spinster with horn-rimmed glasses and a large mound of hair on top of her head.

"I keep seeing refrigerators, washing machines, washing machines, refrigerators, washing machines," Crane said. "Thousands of them, Miss Kirby. Millions of them."

Miss Kirby seemed about to fly from the room.

"They glisten, Miss Kirby. They will not stain or lose their luster. They dress the kitchen, make the basement look like the living room."

40

Under the impression this was a flight of the advertising mind, Miss Kirby began to take notes.

"They're orange juice and ginproof, guaranteed to freeze diapers in ten seconds with the rugged Rapo-Arctic finger-tip, freewheeling action. They have the highest humidity, the lowest frigidity, the greatest rigidity, the finest——

"Miss Kirby, where does a man in my condition go?"

Some of the alarm left Miss Kirby's face.

"Well, Mr Richard March used to go over to the Morgan House taproom about this time in the afternoon. *He* used to say thinking of ice boxes gave *him* chills."

Crane looked at her closely. "Did Mr Richard March come back to the office later?"

"No sir."

Crane seized his coat and hat. "Thank you."

He was followed out of the office by Miss Kirby, who halted to confide to Miss Anselman, the assistant production manager's secretary, that she didn't think Mr Crane was going to do at all.

"He doesn't seem to be serious," she said.

The Morgan House taproom was like home after a long visit with foreigners. It was cool and dim, and there was an odor of limes in the air. He sat in a red-leather upholstered armchair, leaned on a red-lacquered table.

He'd no idea there was so much to manufacturing. He was really confused between the March Rapo-Arctic refrigerator, with the finger-tip blizzard control, and the foam-flinging March Acrobat washer. He had walked down scores of assembly lines, fingered bright parts, nodded wisely to technical lectures on current consumption, shelf features, soap consumption, rinsing, temperature zones, humidity controls, crispers, automatic ironing, fruit storage, clothes capacity, food capacity . . .

He ordered a double scotch and soda. After a time a man came in the taproom and walked up to his table.

"You probably don't remember me," he said. "I'm Doctor Woodrin. I met you at lunch, at the City Club."

"Sure," Crane said. "Sit down. Have a drink?"

The doctor ordered ale. He was a healthy man with a round, pink-and-white face and light blue eyes. His complexion was so fresh it made him look under forty, but Crane was sure he was nearer forty-five.

"After I leave the hospital I drop in for a bottle of ale," Dr Woodrin explained. "I usually run into somebody to gab with."

Crane said, "My secretary told me this was Richard March's afternoon headquarters."

"He used to be here in the morning, too."

"A good idea," Crane said.

After Crane got another scotch and soda they talked. They discussed Marchton. Dr Woodrin said he'd lived in the town for fifteen years. Before that he'd been chief physician for the International Oil Company in Texas and Oklahoma. He was a graduate of Rush Medical, in Chicago. He was now chief of staff at Marchton City Hospital.

"It's a nice position," he said, "but not much money."

Crane, after a time, worked the conversation back to Richard March. He told the physician he had the Richard March house, wanted to know how it happened to be so elaborately decorated.

"That's Alice March," Dr Woodrin said. "You'll understand when you see her. She dresses the same way."

"She divorced him?"

"They were divorced. It was sort of a standoff." He drank the remainder of his ale. "She didn't get any alimony, but was allowed to divorce him. I think Dick's lawyer, old Judge Dornbush, was too smart for Alice's lawyer, Talmadge March."

"Who's Talmadge March?"

"Richard's younger brother." The doctor looked at Crane over his glass. "Their story's like those Greek plays we used to read in college."

Crane took his word for that. Anyway, it was a strange one. Alice had been Talmadge's girl; they were engaged to be married when the handsome Richard met her. The doctor said he supposed it was, for Richard, more the challenge of the engagement, the lure of someone's property, than love; and besides, the brothers had always hated each other.

Marchton's tongue moved a great deal over the elopement, moved less when Alice left Richard five years later, but regained vigor when Talmadge appeared as her attorney in the divorce suit. The gossip reached a climax when, five months before Richard died, the divorce was granted with no settlement, no alimony, Dr Woodrin said. The town wondered what Richard had on his wife. It must have been good; she had plenty on him. There was speculation as to whether Talmadge was involved beyond the role of counsel; it was popularly believed he was still in love with Alice.

"It was a triumph for Talmadge, then," Crane said.

"No. Richard didn't care. He was through with her."

Crane learned Talmadge March was not connected with the March business. He had refused to enter the company, had opened his own law office. He was moderately successful and, the doctor added, he had a large income from the interest his father had left him in the company. It was larger now that Richard was gone.

"That was a funny death," Crane said. "Richard's, I mean."

"It was," Dr Woodrin agreed. "I've often thought about it. You know I was there when he was found."

"You were?"

"I'll tell you about it." The doctor crooked a finger at the waiter. "Two more of the same, Charley."

Crane said, "Let me get these."

Dr Woodrin shook his head at Crane. "It was one of those dry, clear nights in early February," he began. "It was cold, but there was a three-quarter moon. We'd all decided to take a drive after the Country Club dance."

He had come out of the club, he continued, with John March and Carmel, Peter March and Alice and Talmadge, just as the orchestra began to play "Home, Sweet Home." The orchestra had been bad, and they were all glad the dance was over. Alice, who was ahead with Peter, called over her shoulder, "Dick must have passed out."

They could see Richard sprawled over the wheel of his big sedan, his head cradled in his arms; a pale vapor slipping out from under the left-hand running board. The gas was almost the color of milk in the moonlight; Dr Woodrin said. It was like a mist rising over a swamp.

Carmel had called to Peter, ahead: "Dick's engine's on."

Peter went to the sedan and opened the door by the driver's seat, the doctor said, and shook Richard's shoulder. "Come on, old boy," he had said. "Time to go home." He shook him again violently, and said, "Dick!"

Charley, the waiter, put ale and a double scotch and soda on the table, accepted the quarter tip. Crane said, "Thanks."

The doctor said. "Peter sounded scared, and I ran over to him."

They pulled Richard from the sedan, he continued, stretched him on the ground, and he had jerked loose the rear-vision mirror and held it against Richard's lips. It hadn't clouded!

"I knew he was gone, but I sent someone to call an ambulance," Dr Woodrin concluded. "They worked on him at the hospital. He'd been dead for some time."

"Who'd been dead?" a woman's voice asked.

Startled, Crane pivoted to encounter Carmel March's

dark eyes. She was smiling. She wore a gray suit trimmed with blue fox and tailored so that it was tight over sleek hips and high breasts and padded at the shoulders to give them a military appearance. She looked like a Cossack lady.

"Who'd been dead?" she repeated.

Back of her were a man and a woman. Crane knew, at once, that the woman was Alice March. She was blonde and plump, and there was a sweet smile on her face, as though it had been painted there. She was wearing a quantity of jewelry, a silver fox fur and a floppy hat with some imitation blue flowers on it.

"Hello, there," Dr Woodrin said. "Join us?"

It *was* Alice March. The man with her, a middle-sized man with a bored face and languid manners, was Talmadge March. "How d'you do," he said to Crane. He didn't offer his hand.

In response to Crane's invitation, they ordered martinis. Crane had another double scotch and soda with them.

Carmel sat next to Crane. "For the last time, who'd been dead?"

Dr Woodrin said, "I was telling Mr Crane about the former owner of his house."

"The late lamented Richard?" Talmadge inquired.

Crane thought his lightly contemptuous attitude was hardly proper in front of the widow (even the divorced widow), but Alice March smiled sweetly. She seemed pleased.

Carmel asked, "What about Richard?"

"Just the usual story of his death," Dr Woodrin replied.

Talmadge drawled, "I suppose our local Galen told you of the mystery?"

"No," Crane said. "A real mystery?"

"A lady." Talmadge's amused eyes were on Carmel. "A woman, anyway."

"Hell!" said Dr Woodrin. "That mystery's been buried a long time."

"Has it?" Talmadge took a sip of his martini. "I wonder."

Dr Woodrin said, "He's talking about lipstick marks on Richard's face."

"Fresh lipstick," Talmadge drawled. "Naturally there was speculation as to the identity of the lady."

Alice March, her voice sweet, said, "It narrowed down to two or three, I believe."

"Not to you, though, dear," Carmel said.

Crane got an idea the two women didn't like each other.

"The marks looked green," Dr Woodrin said. "I don't know anybody who uses green lipstick."

"I saw them," Talmadge's smile was mocking. "The moon plays strange tricks with colors." He looked directly at Carmel. "But the lady of the green lipstick never came forward."

"She never explained what she was doing," Dr Woodrin said sadly.

"Hell," Crane said. "She must have been kissing Richard."

"A very fine piece of deduction," Talmadge drawled.

"The kiss of death," Crane said. "That's what she was giving him." He liked the phrase. "The kiss of death."

Carmel March's eyes, suddenly jet black, examined his face for a halved second. He grinned foolishly at her. She looked frightened, he thought.

Talmadge said, "There was another clue."

"How do you know so much about this?" demanded Dr Woodrin.

"I was there, and I have eyes . . . and a nose."

Crane gaped at him. "A nose?"

"There was an odor of perfume on Richard's coat." Talmadge's speech was so affected it made him sound feminine. "I caught it as I helped put him in the ambulance—you remember, Woodrin, I lent a hand?"

Woodrin nodded.

"What was the odor?" Crane asked.

"Gardenia perfume."

Carmel said coldly, "You're making that up, Tam."

"Am I, darling?"

Crane got an impression they had forgotten him. He was conscious of an undercurrent of genuine emotion, of a tensity in each of them, with the possible exception of Dr Woodrin. He supposed they ignored him because they thought he was either slightly simple, or drunk. He determined to maintain this impression.

Carmel's face was like a delicately tinted dancer's mask. "You have a lawyer's imagination, Tam." She did not change expression when she talked.

"If I have," Talmadge countered, "how is it you gave up gardenias after Dick died?"

That's done it, Crane thought. Now for an explosion. He wondered why Simeon March hadn't mentioned the gardenia business. He watched Carmel for the eruption, but none came.

She laughed, genuinely amused. "What a fine detective you are!" She leaned toward Crane so that his face was in the hollow formed by her neck and shoulder. "What do you smell, Mr Crane?"

Crane took a deep breath, then said gallantly, "I smell Nassau in May."

"No," she said.

"I smell the Sabine hills after an April rain. I smell flower-strewn boats at Xochimilco. I smell the cherry blossoms of Nippon. I smell a hot tub filled with English bath salts."

Every one laughed except Carmel, who said:

"No, specifically."

Crane said, "I smell gardenias."

Talmadge didn't seem embarrassed. "I thought I might trap you into a confession, Carmel." He grinned at her over his martini. "A lawyer's trick."

"I think it's in pretty poor taste." Carmel remained close to Crane. " . . . If it *was* a joke."

Dr Woodrin was lighting a pipe. "You've a macabre sense of humor, Tam."

Crane was delighted with Talmadge's composure under fire. He liked the name Talmadge March. He acted and sounded like the villains in the 1880 dramas of the New England barn revivals. All he needed was a whip and a pair of handle-bar mustaches.

Talmadge was watching Carmel. "Perhaps it is a bit on the macabre side." She met his eyes angrily, and he looked away. "I'm sorry."

Again Crane felt tension. He asked, "Just what difference does it make who was in the car with Richard before he died?"

"A small town's prurient curiosity," Carmel said bitterly.

"I'm really sorry, Carmel," said Talmadge.

The taproom was beginning to fill, and men and women, as smartly dressed as a New York cocktail-hour crowd, passed by their table. Everybody seemed to know everybody else, and most of the new arrivals either spoke or waved to Crane's companions. The newcomers were very gay and noisy.

"The haut monde of Marchton," Talmadge drawled.

"They look nice," Crane said.

He felt a warm glow about the case. He liked the seductive hollow above Carmel's bare collarbone, the sweet spitefulness of Alice, the name of Talmadge March. He felt sorry for Ann Fortune, sitting at home. He liked the feeling that his expense account was unlimited.

He hoped he would not solve the case too quickly. He wondered if he could be a little drunk.

"One more?" he suggested to the others.

They were perfectly willing. While Charley collected

empty glasses the conversation turned to duck shooting. The season had been open for a couple of weeks, but there hadn't been many birds. The cold weather had made them hopeful for next Sunday's shooting. Talmadge asked Crane if he'd like to shoot with them, and Crane said Peter March had already suggested it.

"It's usually fine shooting," Dr Woodrin said.

For the first time Talmadge spoke without affectation. "Wonderful shooting."

Crane learned that the river lands where the March family and friends shot duck had been acquired by Great-Grandfather March when he emigrated from New England in 1823. He had farmed by the river and died there, and had willed the land as a perpetual estate for the family until there should be no direct male descendants. Then it could be sold.

"Old Jonathan March's idea," Talmadge explained, "was to provide a backlog for the family, a place they could return to when defeated by the outside world."

"He didn't know his grandsons would nick the world for about twenty million dollars," Dr Woodrin said.

"I think it's a nice idea," Crane said. "Is the land worth anything now?"

"About five thousand dollars," Talmadge said.

"It's swell for duck shooting," Dr Woodrin said.

"We wouldn't sell it if we could," Talmadge agreed. "Besides, the doctor wouldn't let us. He's been appointed trustee for the Jonathan March Estate."

"It's a responsible job," Carmel said, smiling. "Administering an estate worth five thousand dollars."

"Five thousand is a lot of money as far as I'm concerned," Dr Woodrin said.

Charley brought them their drinks. Crane was surprised to see Alice March had switched to pernod and water. He had had one unfortunate experience with this substitute for absinthe and he had respect for anyone who could drink it.

Pouring his ale into a tilted glass, Dr Woodrin inquired, "What kind of a shot are you, Crane?"

"I'm fine with a machine gun."

Carmel laughed. She appeared, no doubt because of the martinis, quite gay. "I don't believe we have a machine gunner in Marchton's upper set."

Alice March downed half her pernod, looking as serene as the plump mothers old Italian masters put on canvas. Admiring her fortitude, Crane drank his double scotch.

Carmel said, "I do *my* best work with a pearl-handled automatic."

"That's fine for close work," Crane said. "Nothing like it for a hand-to-hand encounter with a duck."

Alice March said, "Carmel's noted for her close work."

A bellhop in a maroon uniform with two vertical rows of gold buttons halted by the table.

"Mr Crane?"

Crane said, "I believe I am."

"Telephone," the bellhop said.

"Telephone what?"

"For you, sir."

"For me? A telephone? What kind of a telephone?"

"A telephone call, sir."

"How disappointing!" He stood up, made a sweeping bow. "Kindly pardon me." He followed the bellhop.

He heard Talmadge say, "A bit high, I'd say." He heard Dr Woodrin say, "Makes Richard look like a teetotaler." He heard Carmel say, "I like him."

He felt very pleased he had fooled them into thinking he was drunk. He giggled a little at the thought of his cleverness, bumped into a man, said, "Excuse me many times." He carried out his role so thoroughly he had to be helped into the phone booth.

He spoke into the phone. "Crane & Company, novelties, knickknacks, knickers."

It was Ann Fortune. She said, "I thought so."

"I can't help it," he said. "I've been plied with drinks by a mysterious Russian lady."

"I bet."

"And by a man named Talmadge March. He's going to foreclose our mortgage."

Ann said, "I've traced Delia."

"Unhand us, Talmadge March," Crane said.

Ann said, "I've traced Delia."

"Huh? Delia? Oh, Delia. How?"

"Simple deduction."

Crane groaned. "Please. You sound like Philo Vance. Pretty soon you'll be dropping your g's."

"If you come home I'll drive you to the Brookfield house."

"In whose car?"

"Peter March left one here for us."

"For us," Crane repeated ominously. "I suppose you've been roystering with him all afternoon?"

"Why, yes, I have."

"Why isn't he at work?" he demanded. "Why does he have to fiddle around our little dovecot while I freeze, careening from ice cube to ice cube?"

"Aren't you getting your metaphors a little mixed?"

"What's a metaphor, if not to mix?"

There was no answer, and Crane considered the telephone mouthpiece darkly for a moment. "I suppose I can come out. I suppose you called the office and got everybody aware of the fact I wasn't there, anyway."

"I didn't call the office," Ann said.

"But, how did——"

"I simply asked the telephone operator to ring the best bar in town."

CHAPTER V

THAT MORNING, after she had conferred with Beulah about dinner, Ann Fortune put on her black caracul coat, freshened her lipstick and called a taxi.

"The nearest dairy," she told the driver.

This was her first attempt at detection and she felt a little excited. She wondered if the trail would lead her into one of those situations she had so often seen in the William Powell-Myrna Loy movies: possibly to a penthouse with a suave villain from whom she would be saved in the nick of time by the arrival of Bill Crane.

The only trouble was that she felt no confidence in the arrival of Bill Crane anywhere in the nick of time; he was more likely to stop for a drink on the way and come too late.

Not that she didn't like Bill Crane; it was just that he didn't seem to take things seriously. Take the case they were working on: Richard March and John March dead from gas, and Simeon March accusing Carmel, his daughter-in-law, of having murdered them. It was a serious affair! But Bill, apparently, wasn't doing anything about it. He acted as though they were on one of those Long Island house parties he used to take her to in New York when he wasn't working. He acted . . .

"This do, miss?" the driver asked.

It was the Prima Dairy. She smiled a little at the squat white building. It didn't look like the sort of place Myrna Loy would be detecting in.

However, she *did* find out something. Her smile almost disorganized the young clerk who took her order for milk and cream, but he retained possession of enough faculties to tell her that the dairy had the only rural service for Brookfield and Blue Lake in Marchton.

Delia's note telling Richard to shut off milk deliveries must have been written two summers ago since Richard had been dead since February. Ann asked the clerk if he could find a Brookfield account in which the milk had been shut off for a week end around the middle of July of that year.

The clerk discovered that a Saturday two summers ago had come on July nineteenth. Under Delivery Stop Orders on that date he found one for a Raymond Maxwell, 12 February Lane, Brookfield.

Under the *M* file in the regular account book, the clerk found the house on February Lane was owned by a Charles G. Jameson, Brookfield real-estate operator.

Bills had been paid by postal money orders, but there was a letter from Mrs Maxwell, opening the account. Ann's heart jumped when she caught sight of purple ink and Delia's large handwriting.

The clay road to Brookfield was so thickly lined with trees it seemed as though the sedan was going through a long tunnel. Crane brooded over the lecture he had just been given on the evils of strong drink. A warm afternoon sun sent saffron rays angling through elms and oaks and maples, spotlighted bright masses of party-colored leaves. In the air there was a smell of smoke.

He had to admit, though, Ann had done a neat piece of detection in tracing Delia through the dairy. "I guess I owe you a bottle of milk," he said.

"Champagne," Ann said.

"All right. What kind of champagne do you like?"

"Demi-sec, in magnums."

"You'll get it," he said, and added, "I hope it makes you very sec."

This terrible pun made him feel better and he told her what he'd heard in the taproom.

He told her about the discovery of Richard's body, of the lipstick on his face, and of the smell of gardenia on his coat. They wondered why Talmadge March had tried to trap Carmel. Or had it been his idea of a joke?

"I'm beginning to think Richard was having an affair with Carmel," Crane said.

"In addition to our Delia?"

"Richard was a gay dog."

"Do you think Carmel 'd deceive her husband with his first cousin?" Ann asked.

"I don't know."

A break in the tunnel of trees brought them out into bright sunlight. On the right was a black field, stacked evenly with Indian tepees of cornstalks, and dotted with plump, bright pumpkins. A black-and-white calf, chained to a fence post, grazed in the ditch beside the road.

Crane added, "Look at Peter, too. She's quite friendly with him."

"Peter told me this afternoon he wanted to get Richard's letters to protect a lady," Ann said. "From hints he dropped I got the idea the lady is Carmel, and that the letters were important." She glanced at his face. "And that gave me an idea."

The road curved to the right, crossed a small stone bridge and entered a valley. Apple orchards, fruit trees and cornfields lay on either side of them. They passed a wagon loaded with yellow feed corn.

"I think you're wonderful," Crane said.

"Be serious. If Carmel was your wife and was having an affair with Richard, what would you do?"

"I'd lock her up in the coalbin."

"Please be serious."

"I'd be angry with Richard."

"Exactly"

"My God!" Crane blinked at her. "You don't think John killed him?"

"He could have discovered Carmel in the car with Richard (that fits in with the gardenia), sent her into the club, then killed Richard."

"How?"

Ann smiled. "That's as far as I've gone."

"I've got an idea." Crane lit a cigarette, put it in her mouth. "I'll tell you if you're not mad at me."

"I've never been mad at you."

"No?"

"Well, I wish you wouldn't drink so much."

Crane was about to tell her of his plan to make people think he was a drunkard so they'd disregard him, but it didn't sound so convincing sober.

"All right, I won't," he said. "Here's the idea."

He reconstructed the murder (if it had been a murder) for her. Richard, he said, had passed out. Then

John, or someone else, had fastened a rubber hose to the exhaust of his sedan, run the free end through a partially open window, and started the engine. Then, when Richard was dead, he removed the hose.

"I think that's very clever," Ann declared.

The road came to a good cement highway, and Ann turned to the left and increased the sedan's speed. The sun was barely above a long ridge ahead of them, and the air was cooler. Haze hung like muslin over the distant countryside.

Crane was frowning. "Only then I don't see who killed John," he admitted.

Ann held her cigarette out the window to let the wind remove the ash. "John killed himself. Remorse."

Crane looked at her smiling face with respect. "That makes it pretty neat." He pulled the tan camel's hair around him. "But the old man is certain Carmel did the murdering."

Ann said, "That's a good theory, too."

Crane had another thought. "Maybe Carmel signed her notes to Richard with the name Delia."

"She didn't. Her handwriting's different."

"You've been busy, haven't you?"

"One of us has to work."

Crane retired into high dudgeon. He had begun to be

a little alarmed about Ann Fortune. It would be an awful thing if she solved the case singlehanded. He would never live it down. He had a dreadful feeling he might have to go to work.

"I need a drink," he said, and then, as Ann looked at him, added, "of nice warm tea."

Presently he saw they were entering Brookfield. Middle-sized houses, many with fine lawns, sat under great oak and chestnut trees. There were gardens, filled with the yellow and white and orange flowers of late fall, around the houses and barbered hedges around them. Twice the clear stream forced the road to arch its back with stone bridges.

The village had a double main street with a partition of young trees in the middle. The stores had evidently been influenced by Tudor England. Their dark, exposed beams and red bricks contrasted with clean sidewalks and Paris-green grass. A one-story building had two display windows: one read, Daphne Gray, Beautician; the other, Charles G. Jameson, Real Estate.

Ann parked the sedan at an angle to the curb, and they went into the office and found an old man in a pair of slippers tinkering with a radio. He wore a coat and trousers and a shirt, buttoned at the collar, but no tie.

"Fix one o' these?" he demanded.

Crane said he couldn't. He showed the old man a card from the American Insurance Company, said he was an investigator, and asked him about the Maxwells. He didn't know very much about them.

"I recollect they paid Chuck in advance for two years," he said in a reedy voice.

"Then the lease hasn't expired?" Ann asked.

"No, ma'am. They got until next May." He looked curiously at Crane. "What you investigatin', Mr Maxwell's death?"

Crane asked, "How'd you know he'd died?"

"The house ain't been used this summer. And besides, another feller was inquirin' about him last January. I suspicioned he was dead then."

Crane and Ann exchanged glances. Both were thinking Richard March had died soon after the man's inquiries, in February.

"What 'd the man want to know?" Crane asked.

There was a sly look about the old man's bright eyes, as though he shared some secret with Crane. "Wanted to know what Mrs Maxwell looked like."

"Did you tell him?"

"We couldn't. Me and Chuck never laid eyes on her."

"Did he want to know anything else?"

The old man chuckled. "Wanted to know how much

they used the house." He didn't make any noise, just shook inside.

"How much did they?"

The old man gave Crane that sly, secretive look. "It seemed kind of odd. They paid a right fine price for the house." He looked down at his slippers. "But they only came week ends."

Crane asked if he'd seen Maxwell, and he said he had. He thought his name was assumed, but he wasn't sure.

"You've no clue to who he was?" asked Ann.

"Your speakin' of that's a funny thing." The old man looked at her with a pleased smile. "'Bout a month ago I seen a picture that looked a lot like the feller who was askin' for him in January. It was in the newspaper."

"Who was it?"

"John March, the one that died in his garage."

Crane flicked a glance at Ann, then asked, "Do you think Mrs March and Mrs Maxwell were the same person?"

"I got my idears."

Ann was wearing a three-quarter length black caracul coat, fastened at the neck with a gold chain and cut so that it hung like a tunic to just about the knees. She undid the coat and found a photograph in an inside pocket.

"Would you know Mr Maxwell?"

"I reckon so," said the old man.

Crane stared at her with reluctant admiration. He could see it was a photograph of Richard March. Tall, tanned and blond, he looked like a movie actor in gray slacks and an open shirt. Ann handed the picture to the old man, smiled at Crane.

He made a face at her. She was too darned efficient. He thought he had better go to work. He thought it was a fine thing when a man had to work hard to keep ahead of a woman. Especially one as pretty as Ann.

The old man handed back the photograph. "That's him."

"Well, thanks," Crane said.

"One more thing," said the old man, "though I don't know as it's much of a clue . . . "

"It might be," Ann said. "What is it?"

"Well, twice I borrowed matches from Mr Maxwell. An' both times he gave me a package from the Crimson Cat. That's a night club near here."

A middle-aged man with spectacles and dandruff flakes on his blue serge suit came into the office. He turned out to be the old man's son, Charles, who operated the realty business. The old man told him Crane was an insurance investigator, looking up the Maxwells.

"Been a lot of interest in them today," the younger Mr Jameson said.

"How's that?" Crane asked.

"A fellow came a couple of hours ago to collect the Maxwell things. He had a note from Mrs Maxwell."

Ann said excitedly, "He wouldn't still be there?"

"I don't know."

Crane said, "How do we get there?"

Following the younger Mr Jameson's directions, it took them three minutes to reach February Lane. The house was a Cape Cod cottage, white, with a high roof and a screened porch on the side. In the driveway was a big sedan with a woman in the driver's seat.

As Ann brought their car to a stop the woman *booped* the horn. Crane couldn't see her very well, but he got an idea she was young.

A hollow, metallic voice called from the rear of the house, "What's wrong?"

Ann exclaimed, "Our burglar!"

The woman hit the horn again, pushed the starter. Arms bearing a cardboard box, the man came around the house, turned his face toward Crane and Ann, broke into an unsteady run. He jerked open the sedan's door, jumped in as it started. The door swung crazily. He reached out and closed it. The woman gave the motor gas.

"Hey!" Crane called. "Wait a minute."

The car swayed as it entered the street, swung wide around their sedan. Crane caught a vivid impression of the woman. She was handsome with milk-white skin and carrot hair, and her large mouth looked as though it had been lipsticked with a vermilion squirt gun. The man kept his face turned away.

Ann pulled Crane back into the sedan. "Come on."

They got around in a wide sweep which carried them over the curb and onto the soft lawn of a Spanish cottage across the lane. The other car was still in sight. Ann shoved the sedan to fifty-five before she shifted into high. Motor and tires began to scream.

Crane clutched desperately at the dashboard. "Do you think this is a good idea?"

Ann didn't answer. She watched the road, her foot holding the accelerator against the rubber floor mat. Her eyes gleamed and her face was determined. She held the wheel so firmly her knuckles showed white through her skin.

She was a beautiful girl, Crane thought, but he wondered if she didn't have just a shade too much character. She seemed to take the detective business too seriously. She didn't act like a blonde at all. He wondered if she'd been a redhead, too, and had bleached her hair.

With a wail of tires, the sedan rounded a turn. He

looked at the speedometer, saw with horror they were going eighty miles an hour. The other car, swaying violently from one side of the clay road to the other, was about two hundred yards ahead. He hoped his car was more stable, but he suspected it was not. They seemed to be gaining on the other car.

He had to shout to be heard. "What do we do when we catch them?"

"Arrest him. He's a burglar."

"What if he resists?"

"Knock him down."

They were passing through a long valley, and the light was dim. Ann switched on the headlights, but they didn't do much good. The road undulated slightly, and every time they raced over a crest and dropped into the following hollow Crane felt his stomach turn over. It didn't seem to be the road they had come over from Marchton.

Crane shouted, "What if he has a gun?"

"Shoot him."

"With what?"

"In my purse . . . a pistol."

The pistol was a .25 automatic with an effective range of about ten yards. He examined it gingerly, then put it back in the purse.

"You haven't got a drink in there?" he shouted.

She ignored him. She was concentrating on the chase, which was turning out to be a pretty even affair. She drove well, catching the turns with a minimum of slide and seldom allowing the arrow indicator to fall below seventy miles an hour.

The other car had more trouble. On one abrupt curve it slid onto the grass, throwing up a screen of dust, and Crane thought it was going to overturn. He could see suitcases and boxes tumbling about the rear and the man and woman leaning far over to the right, away from the pull of momentum. Almost on the lip of the ditch the car straightened, careened back onto the road.

An instant later Ann hit the turn and Crane held his breath. They made it without trouble.

"Good gal," he said.

He felt a little better. He was beginning to have confidence in her. He was also beginning to feel they would never catch the other car.

Ahead, dark green in the half-light, a wavelike barrier of low hills obstructed the road. The road went up at an easy angle for a half mile, then abruptly made a hairpin turn to the left so that it came back parallel to them, about twenty feet away, but higher. The sedan in front cut almost into the left-hand ditch to make the long turn, taking advantage of the natural banking provided by the ditch. As it came back toward them, not more than thirty yards to the left, Crane could see the woman clinging to the wheel, her face half a foot from the windshield. The man leaned over her back, his head almost out her window, a hand holding a revolver thrust through it. He fired as they passed. Crane ducked at the flash, but he heard no report.

Ann, intent on making the U turn, asked, "What's the matter?"

Crane reached down and turned off the ignition.

"What's the matter?" Ann asked again.

The car lost speed rapidly on the steep grade, came to a stop. They could see the taillight of the other car far up the hill. Presently it disappeared around a bend. There was a sound of crickets from the woods above them.

"We would have caught them," Ann said. "Why did you make me stop?"

Crane turned to the rear seat of the sedan, pointed a finger. In the left-door window, low and to the left, was a neat, thumb-sized hole. The glass around the hole had slivered; it looked like a pineapple ice. The bullet had apparently gone through the open window on the other side. Anyway, they were unable to locate a hole.

CHAPTER VI

THEY DROVE HOME soberly, both preoccupied, and parked the sedan in front of the house.

"How 're we to explain the bullet hole?" Ann asked.

"We could say you shot at me and missed."

She said, "When I do I won't miss."

They went in and found Doc Williams in the kitchen. He was an operative of their agency. He'd driven their car from New York and he was posing as their chauffeur. He was a middle-sized, dapper man with a waxed mustache and a streak of dead-white hair over his left temple. He saluted Crane smartly.

"Have a nice trip?" Crane asked formally.

"Very good, sir."

"Come up to my room. I want to talk with you."

Crane turned to Beulah. "This is Mr Williams. I want you to treat him right."

They mixed a shakerful of martinis in the dining room, then went upstairs.

"How 're you gettin' along with tutz?" Williams asked Crane. He winked at Ann, who was carrying celery, olives, and caviar canapés on a tray.

"I wish she wouldn't keep trying to get into my room at night," Crane said.

"Still got the appeal, hey?"

"It's my silk pajamas," Crane said modestly.

"Next time a burglar comes I'll let him take the ground floor away," Ann declared.

"A burglar?" Doc Williams was interested. "You had a burglar?"

Crane poured the martinis. "First a drink."

The drinks were just right, with the vermouth cutting the flavor of the gin without destroying the dryness. Crane poured a second round, then told of the burglary, of Mr March's accusation of Carmel March, of Delia and of the recent chase.

Williams was pleased. "It looks as though we're in for something."

"You'll think so when you see Carmel."

"A good number?"

Crane said, "Just looking at her makes me wish I knew how to tango."

The caviar was excellent. The black eggs were the size of buckshot, and about half the canapés had grated onion sprinkled over them. Some of the celery was stuffed with Roquefort.

Williams smiled at Ann. "It looks to me like you was giving Uncle William some lessons in detection."

"I am," Ann said.

Crane finished his drink, poured another. "I was afraid you were going to mention that." He selected a heart-shaped canapé.

"Yes, and where's my champagne?" Ann said.

"You'll get it . . . probably across the bow, too, the way they christen a ship."

They sipped the martinis, munched celery and discussed the case. They agreed they would visit the Crimson Cat on the following night. Ann went to her room and presently reappeared in a semiformal dress of blue brocaded lamé with silver shoulder straps. Her skin was smooth and tan.

Williams removed an olive pit from his mouth, flicked it under Crane's bed. "Bill was saying John traveled for the company, Ann."

"Yes?"

"That 'd give Richard a chance to chase Carmel."

"And John knew it," Crane added. "Or else he wouldn't have inquired about Richard's dovecot from the Jamesons."

Ann sat on the arm of Williams' chair. "But where did he hear about the cottage?"

Crane didn't know.

"He couldn't have heard much," Williams asserted. "He wouldn't have asked the Jamesons to describe the woman if he had."

Crane admired Ann's eyes, quite green under artificial light. He said, "We agreed John found out about Richard and Carmel and killed Richard to stop the affair."

"But who killed John?" Williams objected.

"We thought of that," Ann said. "He killed himself in remorse."

"What about Carmel?" Williams asked Crane, who was furtively tilting the shaker over his glass.

"I think she's beautiful," he replied.

Ann asked, "You're not going to get tight again, Bill?"

"Oh no." The shaker was empty, anyway. "Not me."

"I mean," Williams said, "couldn't Carmel have killed her husband?"

"Why?"

"She loved Richard, she wanted to avenge him."

Crane picked the olive out of his glass. It had absorbed enough alcohol to taste good. "Old man March thinks she killed him. He thinks she killed them both."

Williams asked, "Does he think she's going to wipe out the whole family . . . one by one?"

"Gosh!" Crane said. "I didn't ask him."

After dinner, Beulah's brother, James, served Ann and Crane coffee and brandy in the library before a bright pine fire.

"I don't like being a detective," Ann said.

Crane was astonished. "What could be nicer than this?" He halted his demitasse halfway to his mouth. "And besides, it isn't costing us a cent."

"It's a dead man's house," Ann said.

"Are you afraid of ghosts?"

"I don't know what it is." She looked at him through very wide green eyes. "I think it's the way everybody dies. Doesn't it give you a creepy feeling, Bill?"

"I haven't had a creep yet, darling."

"I think it's the gas. It hasn't any odor or color; it just sneaks up and kills you. It's horrible. Thinking of it makes me feel it in my throat, choking off my breath."

"Don't think about it, then," Crane said.

"If I were a March I'd be scared to death." Light from the fire made her eyes glisten. "It's like having a curse on a family. So much hatred and death . . . "

"You aren't a March," Crane said.

She was silent.

After a few minutes James brought Peter and Carmel into the library. Carmel took off her glossy mink coat, tossed it carelessly across the library couch. "Hello." Her voice had a throaty quality. She sat on the couch, crossed her legs. They were slender and long, but rounded.

"Hello," Crane said.

She had on a black velvet evening gown, so simple and so perfectly fitted to her body, that Crane knew it must have cost a lot of money. A diamond-and-ruby bracelet, on her left arm, glittered in the rays of the pine fire.

Ann greeted Peter. "How's the burglary business tonight?"

His face was pleasant with a smile. "I never start work before midnight."

"Then have a drink," Crane said.

James brought cups and fragile inhalers, and Ann poured them coffee from a chromium pot with an arched nose. Crane gave them good portions of brandy. Ann sat in a leather chair. Crane decided her legs were as attractive as Carmel's. They weren't so long, but the knees were better.

Peter said, "What we came over for was . . . "

Crane interrupted him. "I know. You came for your car."

"Oh no."

"It's slightly damaged but it runs," Crane persisted.

"A pebble flew up and made a hole in the window," Ann explained.

"No, it was a bullet," said Crane.

"A passing car." Ann glared at him. "A stone must have shot up from its tires."

"It was an obvious attempt to assassinate us both." Crane said. "I was terrified."

While Ann poured the brandy Carmel said, "What we really came over for was to tell you about the Country Club dance Saturday night." Crane smelled her gardenia perfume.

"I told you Dad fixed you up with a membership," Peter said. "We thought you might like to come with us."

"That's awfully nice of you," Ann said.

"I only dance the bunny hug," Crane said. "Has that got out here yet?"

"Oh yes." Carmel smiled at him. "We do that and the subway dip and turkey in the straw."

"Then I'll come," said Crane decisively. "But you'll

have to come to the Crimson Cat with me tomorrow night."

"I think that would be splendid," Carmel said.

They drank some more and soon Crane found himself sitting on the davenport with Carmel. Ann and Peter were in the kitchen. Carmel's skin was very pale, but it had a warm undertone of health; he thought she was a remarkably seductive woman. There was insolence about the arch of her dark brows, passion in her scarlet lips, a contemptuous abandon in the curve of her body on the couch. She had the violet-shaded hollows under her cheekbones Crane admired so much in women.

"Do all the corpses in Marchton smell of gardenias?" he asked.

Her eyes widened for an instant. "What do you mean?" Then they looked directly into his. "Oh, you're remembering this afternoon."

"Yes."

"Talmadge has a malicious tongue."

"But your husband, someone told me he smelled of gardenias," he lied.

Anger brought a faint glow to her eyes. "Why shouldn't he? After all, he was my husband." She leaned toward him so that the gardenia odor was strong in his nostrils. "Who told you?"

"Someone."

"You won't tell?"

"I don't think I better."

"I can guess." She looked at him and he imagined he saw fear and anger in her eyes. "I can guess."

"You have some enemies." He would have liked to know who she was thinking of, but he didn't dare press the matter further. He wanted her to believe he actually knew something.

She was looking at him again. "Why are you so interested?"

"I don't know," he said. "I am, though."

She spoke slowly. "You're thinking there's something back of Richard's and John's deaths."

"Perhaps."

"Well, you're right. There is."

He stared at her in silence, hiding his excitement.

"I might as well tell you before you stir up trouble." Her voice was flat. "John March killed himself."

"But why . . . " he began, and stopped suddenly as Peter and Ann came from the kitchen. He began again, "But why don't they hold the dances at the Town Club?"

"The ballroom isn't as large," Carmel said.

Peter's voice sounded young. "I'm going to scram,

give you a chance to get some sleep. Crane's got to be at the office on the dot or Dad 'll think he's a loafer."

"What office?" Crane demanded.

Ann said, "You may not remember, darling, but you're employed by March & Company to write about refrigerators."

Crane groaned. "For a happy moment that fact had completely slipped my mind."

Peter asked, "Coming, Carmel?"

"You take your car and I'll walk home. I want to have a word with Mr Crane." She glanced at Ann. "That is, if Mrs Crane doesn't mind?"

"Of course I don't," Ann said.

"Well, I'll be off," Peter said.

Ann followed him out.

Crane asked, "How do you know he killed himself?"

"He left a note."

"He did!" Crane didn't have to act; he was really surprised. "What did it say?"

"I can remember it exactly." Carmel's fingers pulled at the diamond-and-ruby bracelet. "It was written to me. It said: '*I can't go on . . . I've got to see Richard . . . explain to him . . . good-by, darling . . . forgive me as I've forgiven you.*'"

"My gosh!" Crane's mind sifted the implication of the note. "Was it signed?"

"Yes. With a *J*. That's the way John signed all his private letters."

"But why wasn't the note brought out at the inquest?"

"I destroyed it." Her words came out jerkily, as though she had been running and was out of breath. "I wanted it to look like an accident."

"Insurance?"

She glared at him, really angry for the first time. "Do you think that would make any difference? What kind of a woman do you suppose I am?" Her breath made a rushing noise in her throat. "It was his father. . . . It would have killed him to know John was a suicide."

Crane, surprised, asked, "*You* worried about Simeon March?"

"Oh, I know he hates me." She laughed briefly, without humor. "He wanted John to bury himself in work, to live for March & Company. I . . . I had other ideas." For a moment her face was tragic. "Simeon March keeps a shell of rage and hate and hard words about him, but he can be hurt inside. He loved John. I didn't want to make him suffer. God knows there's been enough already."

She was either acting beautifully, or her emotion was genuine. Her slender fingers plucked at the rubies on the bracelet. Her face was still masklike, but her glistening, red lower lip trembled.

He asked, "What gave you the idea of destroying the note?"

"After I'd found John, I called Paul . . . Dr Woodrin. He thought, at first, it was an accident." She had turned her face away from him, was talking in a low voice. "That gave me the idea."

"Did you show him the note?"

She hesitated. "Yes. He agreed that it should be destroyed, to avoid a scandal and to save Simeon March. He helped me fix the tools . . . close the garage doors to make it look accidental."

Crane thought of the bizarre twist her story gave the case. Carmel, risking a great deal to protect Simeon March from the knowledge that his favorite son had killed himself. And Simeon, convinced she had murdered John.

He said, "What did John's note mean, 'I've got to see Richard . . . explain to him'?"

A tiny blue vein fluttered at the base of her throat with each beat of her heart. She took a long time, then said in a flat expressionless voice, "John killed Richard."

Crane got off the couch and put a chunk of pine on the fire. Sparks flew up the chimney, tongues of flame licked the fresh wood. He went back to the couch.

"Why?" he asked.

"He was jealous of Richard."

"Yes, but a man doesn't"—he hesitated over the next word—"murder because he's jealous."

"No."

"Then what——"

"He saw me with Richard in his car."

"At the Country Club? On the night of Richard's death?"

She nodded, her face still turned away from him. He understood, then, the smell of gardenia on the dead man's coat, the lipstick on his face.

She went on, speaking slowly, "John must have come up to the car very quietly. I don't know how long he'd been there." Her low voice sounded as though she had not come to the end of a sentence, had only paused.

Crane waited, but she didn't go on. He asked, "He overheard you talking?"

"Richard was begging me to go away with him."

"Was John terribly angry? Did he make any threats?"

She was facing him on the couch now, her face completely unguarded. Her lips were soft and moist and red.

"He was very quiet . . . I couldn't see his face. He asked me to go into the clubhouse. I should have been afraid, his voice was so strange, but I went in . . . left him there with Richard."

"And then——"

"The next thing I knew Richard was dead."

Crane was surprised to see tears rolling in big, slow drops down her cheeks. It was very strange. She didn't sob or move in any way; she just sat there, her face like ivory, talking and letting those big tears roll down her cheeks.

"I never talked to John about it," she went on. "I was never sure . . . until I found his body."

"How do you suppose he killed Richard?"

"I don't know." Tears made her black eyes luminous. She pulled her mink coat from the back of the couch. "I think Richard must have passed out; he had too much champagne, and John did something to the car." She found a lace handkerchief, held it to her eyes. "I'm sorry."

"I know," he said. "Your husband's death must have been a shock."

"It wasn't as if I'd loved him." She looked at him over the handkerchief. "We hadn't been getting along." Her eyes had changed from black to amber.

"You cared for Richard?"

"I liked him, but I didn't love him."

She spoke so simply that Crane believed her. He believed her entire story. He wondered if he did because she was so beautiful. He thought he would make a hell of a juror if she were on trial. He'd let her go with a vote of confidence.

The tears had stopped; she put the handkerchief back in the mink coat. "You think I'm horrible."

"No, I don't."

"You must."

"I really don't."

She touched his wrist for an instant with the tips of her fingers. "Thanks. I had to tell somebody." He felt goose flesh rise all over him. "There was nobody in town I could talk to." She stood up and he held the mink coat for her.

"You won't . . . " she began.

"Of course not."

"Say good night to your wife for me."

"I'll take you home."

"Don't bother."

"But . . . "

"I'd rather go alone."

They were at the front door. "Well, then, good night."

"Good night . . . and thanks."

CHAPTER VII

THE LIMOUSINE traveled the winding road at a good speed, and without strain climbed a long grade. So bright was the moon that the rays from the headlights looked like spilled milk on the cement. The countryside was gray and black.

Dr Woodrin, between Ann Fortune and Carmel March on the back seat, commented on the car's power.

Crane and Peter March were on small seats facing the other three. Crane lied: "I wrote some advertisements for the company. They gave it to me."

"I should 've taken up advertising," Dr Woodrin said.

Carmel said, "You could have a private tennis court then, Paul."

While Peter explained to Ann that Dr Woodrin's chief enthusiasm was tennis Crane thought over the day, decided he had accomplished exactly nothing. The party was bound for the Crimson Cat, with Williams driving, and he hoped he would find something there.

He hadn't even told Simeon March about Carmel's

story of Richard's murder and her husband's suicide. He knew the old man wouldn't believe it, and he wasn't sure he did himself, now that he'd thought it over. The tools and the lifted hood on John's car puzzled him. How had she had the courage to set the stage for the police, with her husband's body lying there? The natural thing would be to call for help at once.

Of course her story, if true, did tie everything. . . .

"Do you play tennis, Bill?" Peter March asked him.

"Huh? Oh, a little."

Ann said she did, and Crane returned to his thoughts. If Carmel's story wasn't true it meant that John had been murdered. She wouldn't bother to lie if the death had been accidental. It was either suicide or murder.

He felt his heart beat accelerate. Murder made it a real case, with plenty to worry about. It was a spooky way the victims died, without a struggle or a call for help, just being eased out of life by a gas that left their faces purple and their blood filled with poison. And if it was murder it meant someone wanted to get rid of the March family. It meant there would probably be another attempt on a March. He hoped it wouldn't be Carmel. He felt she was interesting.

"Paul even carries a tennis net in his car," Peter said. "I saw it the other day."

"Why not?" Dr Woodrin demanded. "The hospital courts don't have nets."

And the scent of gardenias . . . How did that fit into the case? That was a creepy angle, Crane thought. It looked as though someone wanted to implicate Carmel. And why was Talmadge March so eager to establish the odor? Just being with someone didn't leave a smell of gardenias about them. Or did it?

Carmel asked, "Bill, you're not asleep?"

"What? Me? Oh no."

"You're so silent."

Ann said acidly, "His edge has worn off."

Crane didn't like that. Maybe he'd had a few too many cocktails before dinner but he'd been a gentleman. He said, "I hope we're not getting a dose of carbon monoxide."

This was not the right thing to say. Peter March hastily pointed out the left window. "Down there," he said, "you'll see our fair city."

Street lights crisscrossed a spot on the valley below them, made the whole valley look like a velvet setting for an intricate pattern of diamonds. The limousine was no longer climbing. The city looked small and compact.

"Only two miles," Peter said.

Carmel's face, faintly illuminated by the light from

the dash, looked sad. Her cheeks were hollow and her red lips had a tragic downward curve. "That's good," she said. "I need a drink."

"Me, too," Crane said.

He had, at that, done one thing during the day. Or rather, Williams had. He'd located both Richard's and John's cars. It would be interesting to examine them, to see if they had been tampered with. That might show . . .

A swerve of the car interrupted him again. They had turned into the driveway leading to the night club. The white cement building was large and had a Spanish appearance. There was a row of small balconies in front of the upstairs windows. A big red cat, with an arched back and a fuzzy tail, was formed by neon lights over the entrance.

"They've a hot band here," Dr Woodrin said.

There was no doorman. Crane helped the women out. Carmel's hand, in his for an instant, was hot. He let the others start into the club.

Williams eyed Carmel's ankles, slender and seductive, under her mink coat. "I'd like to get trapped in an elevator with that dame," he said.

Crane said, "You do and the newspapers 'll have a story headed: New Carbon-Monoxide Victim."

"You think she's the one?"

Crane shrugged his shoulders. He went into the building and checked his coat and hat. He started for the main room, but went by mistake into a taproom with modern tables made of chromium and glass, red leather chairs and a bright red bar. He paused for a double scotch and soda.

"Doing a good business?" he asked the bartender.

The bartender had two gold teeth. "Wouldn't you like to know, pal?" he said.

Crane let the matter drop and found the main room. He could see Peter March and Dr Woodrin at a table by the dance floor. He felt better because of the whisky. He stood and watched the Negro orchestra come through a door in back of the stand. He wondered if he ought to go back and sock the bartender. He guessed not.

A pretty blonde in a cheap evening gown stopped him on his way to the table. "Alone?" She looked about seventeen years old.

"Practically," he said, "except for a wife."

"Oh, excuse me."

He took her arm. "Come on." If Ann was going to be nasty he'd give her something to be nasty about. "We've got an extra man." He grinned at her. "He'll take care of my wife."

"All right." A closer inspection showed she was more mature than he thought. "At least for a while. Later I got to dance."

"I'll dance with you."

"No. I mean in the floor show. I do a specialty."

"Every woman should have a specialty," he said.

"I tap-dance," she said.

"I think that's nice. And here are our friends." He bowed to Peter March and Dr Woodrin. "This little lady is going to sit with us for a short time and partake of champagne."

"If it's champagne I may sit for a long time." She sat down by Dr Woodrin. "My name's Dolly Wilson."

"Mine's Bill Crane." Crane waved for a waiter. "These are Mr March and Doctor Woodrin."

Miss Wilson gaped at Peter March. "Say!" she exclaimed. "I thought you was dead."

"I'm not, though," Peter said.

"Well, that's funny. You were out here a couple of times a year or so ago, and then I heard you were dead."

"That was my brother. We looked very much alike."

"Oh, say!" She reached over and squeezed his hand. "I'm awful sorry, Mister March."

"That's all right."

Carmel and Ann came to the table. All over the room

people stared at them; the women looking at their clothes, the men at their faces. From even a few feet away Carmel was much the more striking, with dead-white skin, tomato-red lips and jet-black hair.

But Ann, Crane thought, was best quite near. Her tan skin was flawless; her eyes had interesting green depths. Her hair was the color of sun-dried bamboo. She was pretty even when she was angry.

He tried to hold her chair for her, but Peter March got to it first. He introduced Dolly Wilson to the women.

Dr Woodrin, his eyes twinkling, said, "An old friend of Crane's."

Crane said, "She nursed me back to health after the battle of Gettysburg."

This set Miss Wilson to giggling. It was awfully funny because how could she have nursed him after the battle of Gettysburg? She was only nineteen and she must have been a little girl then. It was awfully funny.

Peter had already ordered champagne, and the waiter poured it into hollow-stemmed glasses. "Here's how," Crane said.

They drank. Ann pointedly ignored Crane, carried on a quiet conversation with Peter March. They seemed to like each other, Crane thought. Well, all right. The orchestra started a slow fox trot and he asked Miss Wilson if she would like to dance.

"And how!" she said.

She danced very well. For a time she was wary, watching for a false move of one kind or another on his part, but she soon came closer to him, closed her eyes, put a cheek against his.

"You're not bad," she said.

"I'm wonderful."

She had to giggle at this. Imagine his saying he was wonderful! He was awfully funny. She wondered which one was his wife. She hoped it wasn't the haughty-looking brunette. She was swell looking, all right, but she looked as though she'd be tough to live with. The blonde looked nice.

"Who runs this joint?" Crane asked.

"Frenchy Duval," she said. "But he doesn't own it. It's one of Slats' places."

He recalled the "Slats" of Delia's letter to Richard. "Slats who?"

"Slats Donovan."

"Who's he?"

"Oh, you've heard of him."

"No, I haven't."

"You must have. He runs the gambling in this district. *You've* heard of him."

"I've heard of Al Capone."

"Oh, you!"

The orchestra, according to a bass drum lit with red bulbs, was Sammy Parson's Swing Seven, but the members didn't work very hard at whatever they were playing. They had a good sense of time, though, and the music was good, if a little brassy.

"They don't jam until after the last show," Dolly explained.

Crane caught sight of a woman who had just come out from behind magenta drapes at the orchestra end of the room. She was wearing a black velvet evening gown which clung to her body as tightly as a wet bathing suit. She had fine curves but she wasn't fat. She had carrot-red hair.

Crane danced in her direction. "Who's that dame?"

"Which one? Oh! Delia Young."

Crane's stomach tingled. It was the Delia of the letters. And the redhead of the chase. And Slats was Slats. He wondered if she would recognize him, and danced closer. Her eyes passed over him casually, went to other couples on the floor.

"What's she do?" he asked.

"She sings. She's good. They say she makes two hundred dollars a week."

Crane showed great surprise for Dolly's benefit.

"I'd like to meet her."

Dolly was alarmed. "No, you wouldn't."

"Why?"

"She's Slats' girl."

"Couldn't I buy her a drink?"

"Listen." Dolly moved back a few inches, looked in his face. "The last guy who bought her a drink—they found him dead of an oversupply of mineral."

"Mineral?"

"He had too much lead in his body." She giggled. "I got you on that."

"Well, well." He looked longingly at Delia Young's curves. "Slats is jealous, hey?"

"With reason." Dolly's young face was wise. "She gets a few slugs under her girdle and thinks it's Christmas."

Crane was bewildered. "Christmas?"

"Yeah. She gets into the spirit of giving things away."

"Oh. And Slats doesn't like that?"

"What man would? He even went so far as to give her a bodyguard."

"A sort of walking chastity belt, hey?"

"Huh?"

"That's one I got *you* on," Crane said. "Does the guy talk as though he had a bad needle on his phonograph?"

She jerked away from him, stopped dancing. "Say! What do you know?"

Other dancers began to look at them. "Nothing," he said. "I remembered someone in Marchton telling me about her, that's all."

She allowed him to dance with her again, but her face was suspicious. "You've never seen her before?"

"Never," he lied.

"If Slats heard me telling this I'd get my teeth knocked out."

"He's tough?"

"I seen him put his fist through a door once." She squeezed his arm. "I gotta go. The show starts in five minutes. Keep out of trouble until I get back."

"I will," he promised.

He walked back to the table. Carmel and Dr Woodrin were there alone. Carmel said, "We thought you had gone for the evening."

"The evening's young yet," Crane said.

He sat down and looked for Ann and Peter, but they weren't dancing. He felt a trifle angry. Ann was supposed to be his wife, even though she wasn't. He drank some of his champagne. He decided to watch for an opportunity to meet Delia Young. He didn't know whether he was going to do it to pursue his investigations, or to annoy Ann. He guessed he didn't much care.

CHAPTER VIII

"BRINGING a strange girl to the table," Ann said, dancing as far away from him as possible. "A pickup!"

"So that's what's the matter," Crane said.

"No, it isn't."

"Then why are you angry?"

"I'm not."

It was the last dance before the floor show. Ann had come back with Peter March and Crane had asked her to dance. She hadn't seemed enthusiastic, but she went out on the floor with him.

"I guess I'm glad I'm not married to you," he said.

"Not half as glad as I am."

"I'm not really glad," he said. "I think you're swell. But don't you see I have to work?"

"Do you call drinking and chasing after girls working?"

"Certainly."

"How do you think I feel, having a husband on the loose?"

"But we're not married."

"People think we are." Her voice was cold. "I don't like people thinking they have to be nice to me because you aren't."

"You mean Peter?"

She looked at him scornfully. "He's been very thoughtful."

"I'm thoughtful, too. But I have to work."

The orchestra was playing an old piece which Crane remembered Paul Whiteman as having played. It was a fairly fast piece, with lots of work for saxophones and trumpets, and it was hard to dance and talk. He thought the name of it was "You Took Advantage of Me." He caught sight of Delia Young's red hair in a corner of the room. She was talking to a man in a black suit.

"Would you want me to slight my work?" he asked.

She didn't answer and when he looked at her he was surprised to see moisture in her green eyes. He felt a tingling sensation in his stomach. He supposed it was sympathy. He felt a desire to hold her tight against his chest. That was sympathy, too.

"I'll quit work," he said. "I'll be nice."

"It's nothing to me what you do," she said.

She pushed his arms away and stopped dancing and left him. She held herself very stiff in walking.

He wondered why she had done that. It made him a little mad.

He went into the taproom and had a double scotch and soda. He saw Williams at the end of the red bar, in conversation with the tough barman, but he ignored him. Presently Peter March came in and sat on the next stool.

"Have a drink?" Crane said.

"Sure."

Crane ordered two more double scotch and sodas.

"Aren't you drinking quite a lot?" Peter March said.

"Not so much."

"Ann . . . your wife doesn't like it very well."

"So I gathered."

"She's a nice girl."

"So am I," Crane said. "I'm a nice girl."

"Sure. But I just thought . . ."

"Don't. Don't ever think."

"Maybe you're right," Peter March said reflectively. "It's none of my business. But there is something that is." He paused and eyed Crane. "There *was* a bullet in my car."

"Sure," said Crane. "I told you."

"But how did it get there?"

"I don't know."

There was authority in Peter March's voice. "I think you'd better tell me."

"All right," Crane said. "Ann tried to kill me. She wants my millions. But my steel vest deflected the bullet."

Peter's brows were straight lines above his eyes. He looked as though he would like to hit Crane. Then he saw Dr Woodrin coming toward them. "O.K.," he said. He got up and left him.

"Have a drink?" Crane asked Dr Woodrin when he came up.

The doctor had a scotch and soda, too.

"Say!" Crane said when the bartender had left them. "I've just heard something strange from Carmel. I think I'd better tell you since you're involved."

"What is it?"

Crane told him Carmel's story of John's suicide. "Was there really a note?" he asked.

Dr Woodrin's pink-and-white face was serious. "Gosh! I hoped that wouldn't get out." His blue eyes searched Crane's face. "How'd she happen to tell you?"

"She was angry at Talmadge March."

"I don't blame her. . . . I don't know what he was driving at yesterday."

"I guess he doesn't like her," Crane said.

"That's Alice's work." The doctor shook his head. "Alice hates Carmel."

"Because of Richard?"

"Partly, and partly just because they're different breeds of cats."

"And there was a note?" Crane persisted.

"Yes." The doctor drained his glass. "Her story's true." He slid off his stool. "I hope you won't say anything about it, though."

"I won't," Crane said.

"I'd be in trouble if the police found out. I helped to make it look accidental," Dr Woodrin said. "And it would kill Simeon March." He walked away.

After a time Crane went back to the table. The show had started and six girls in blue silk panties and glass-encrusted brassières were dancing. They were very bad. Crane recognized Dolly Wilson at the left end. She waved at him. Ann was back at the table with the others, and he sat beside her. She paid no attention to him.

He felt a little bit lonely. Nobody liked him except Dolly Wilson. It was tough, being a detective and having nobody but Dolly Wilson like you. He felt possibly he was a little drunk. That was good, but he wished he had someone around who liked him and who . . . and *whom* he liked. That was good grammar. Damn good grammar! He liked Ann, but she didn't like him. He didn't like the floor show, and he didn't care whether the floor show liked him or not. That was immaterial. Absolutely. He didn't like Peter March. He tried to look at Dr Woodrin to see if he liked him, but his chair overbalanced and Carmel March had to catch him.

"Thank you," he said to Carmel. "You have saved my life."

"I didn't do anything," Carmel said.

"You saved my life."

Ann said, "Be quiet."

A moment later he didn't have to be urged to be quiet. The lights went out, the orchestra began to moan, a circle of chalk light sought out Delia Young by the magenta curtains. She moved slowly, exaggerating the swing of her curved hips, to the center of the floor. Her skin was as white as bathroom tile.

She looked as though she were half asleep. Her eyes were almost closed. The piano hit a few chords. She sang:

> "*I'm not much to look at;*
> *Nothing to see. . .*"

Cold shivers coursed along Crane's back. Her voice was like no other voice he had ever heard. It was husky-hoarse, but in a feminine way; it was as though she had a cold, as though she had tuberculosis of the larynx. But the voice had range and control, rising to an icy vibrancy which made Crane's ears shudder, then falling to a dry whisper that people held their breath to hear.

The piece was a very sad one. The tempo was slow; the accompaniment of drum, piano and violin subdued. Delia Young sang:

> "*I got a fellow crazy for me,*
> *He's funny that way. . . .*"

She finished the verse, stood in the spotlight with closed eyes. Back of her the orchestra swung it with trumpets, clarinet and saxophones. It made a hell of a contrast; it was a very fine effect. Then the piano took the break again, very slow, and the husky, magic voice poured from Delia Young's lips.

Her face was expressionless, sleepy, bored; her breast hardly moved; it was as if she, through no volition of her own, simply opened her mouth and let the melancholy song come out.

There was no clapping immediately after she finished. Then there was a lot, but she wouldn't sing again. She glided behind the curtains; the lights went on; Dolly Wilson began to tap-dance with more energy than skill.

Carmel smiled at Crane. "Sings well, doesn't she?"

"My God!" Crane said.

After a while he saw Delia Young seated alone at a table diagonally across the dance floor. He had the waiter bring a bottle of champagne in an ice bucket, tied to the bottle a card on which he had written: "If you want help with this I am ready."

The waiter hesitated. "I'm not sure Miss Young will appreciate this. You know she's . . ."

"So I've heard." Crane gave him a five-dollar bill. "Don't let it worry you."

Ann was also looking at Delia. She turned to Crane, "If you're not too tight will you tell me something?"

"Darling, I'm not a bit tight."

"Is that our Delia?"

He nodded his head. The floor show ended and the orchestra began to play dance music. Ann smiled at Peter March and he took her onto the floor. She didn't look at Crane. The waiter brought a note. It read: "Bring your own bottle."

He was genuinely amused. That was a smart one. He'd sent her a bottle, but apparently he had no interest in it. "Send Miss Young another bottle," he told the waiter. He thought he was going to like Delia.

He got up and said to Carmel and Dr Woodrin, "Please forgive me."

"Why?" Carmel asked.

"I've been invited to a small reception . . . a very small reception in honor of Miss Young."

Carmel drawled. "She's said to be the gal of the toughest guy in these parts."

"Please forgive me," Crane said.

He had trouble crossing the dance floor. There seemed to be a great many people on the floor, and all of them had to bump into him. Some of them had to bump into him twice. The thing was that if the floor hadn't been tilted up in the direction of Delia Young's table he wouldn't have had to walk bent over and consequently could have avoided the couples who bumped him. But he couldn't avoid them, and for a time he considered getting on hands and knees and crawling under the couples and up the incline. Suddenly he found himself by her table.

Her eyes were purple and amused. "The sea rough?"

He sat opposite her. "Would you care to dance?"

"Do you think you can, mister?"

He stood up, bowed, caught his balance by clutching the table. "Excuse!" He bowed, caught his balance by clutching a chair. He gave up trying to bow. "Madam, please meet the greatest little dancer of them all."

Delia Young slid back her chair. "Remember, Arthur Murray, I leave you where you fall."

They walked to the floor and danced, and it was quite a surprise to everybody.

It surprised Delia Young because he danced very well, and it surprised Crane because he hadn't expected her to dance with him. It surprised Frenchy Duval, watching from the door and thinking it was a good thing Slats Donovan was not there, because ordinarily when Delia had a snootful she didn't exactly dance that way. It surprised Dolly Wilson, who had taken off her tap shoes expecting to dance with Crane. And it surprised Ann, though not very much.

When the orchestra stopped, Crane walked fairly steadily back to the table, held the chair for Delia Young. She looked at him curiously as he sat down. "You're not bad, Arthur."

"No, I'm not."

The waiter poured champagne. He filled Delia's glass only halfway, but she called him back. "What's the idea? Frenchy trying to taper me off?" He filled it to the brim.

They drank and then danced. Then they drank. Crane thought she was a splendid woman. "I think you are a splendid woman," he said.

"I'm high, wide and handsome," she said. "I'm tall."

"Tall?"

"High. Tight. Crocked. Drunk."

"Oh, tall?" Crane had never before heard this word. It was a good one. He said, "Champagne always makes me tall."

"Did you ever try gin and laudanum?"

"Gin and laudanum always makes me tall."

"Did you ever try champagne and laudanum?"

"No."

"Never champagne and laudanum, Arthur?"

"No. Did you?"

"No."

Her black dress was cut in such a way that when she stood up only about one half of her breast was exposed, but when she bent over the table he could see she wasn't wearing a brassière. She noticed his eyes, but she didn't bother to sit upright.

"You know whose girl I am, Arthur?"

"Sure. Mine."

Her laughter was mocking, throaty. It came from way down in her chest. It was deep. It sounded as though it would bring up phlegm.

"I wish I was," she said.

"Don't you like Slats?"

"He's all right, but he don't know what a woman wants."

"I thought he gave you plenty of do-re-me."

"Don't be smart."

"I'm not."

"I'm not talking about cash."

He nodded his head wisely. People were dancing near their table. A jigaboo was singing, "I'll always hear that melody . . ." The orchestra was finishing "Star Dust." A waiter filled their glasses. What was she talking about? Oh yes. She was talking about not talking about cash.

"Any dame, even one like me, wants love," Delia Young said seriously.

"Have you ever been in love?" Crane asked.

She nodded her carrot-red head.

"That's nice."

"Like hell." She leaned toward him, and he modestly averted his eyes. "It hurts."

"You picked the wrong guy?"

"I'd pick him again if I had the chance."

"Why haven't you?"

"He's dead."

"Oh. What was his name?"

Her purple eyes studied his face. Her skin had the color, the smooth appearance of very rich milk: it was the kind of skin that went out of favor with the Gibson Girl. She had large, beautiful shoulders.

"If it's any of your Goddamn business," she said, "it was Richard March."

Crane put a great deal of disbelief in his voice. "*You* knew him?" Here was his chance to learn something.

"You don't think I did, Arthur?"

"Who am I to doubt a lady?"

"Get this." Her crimson mouth was grim. "I'm no lady, but I knew Richard, all right."

He tried to get further revelations from her. "I bet you wrote him mash notes."

"Would you like to have your throat cut, Arthur?"

"No," he said. "I'd rather dance."

The orchestra was playing "Sugar" and the trombone player was having a jam for himself. The other black boys in the orchestra showed white teeth and eyeballs in appreciation. The dancers moved about the floor rapidly, and they smiled, too.

Crane said, "That's the tonic."

Delia said, "Wasn't you with that party over there?"

Crane looked, but all he could see was a vacant table. "What party over there?"

"The one that left a half-hour ago."

"If they left I am not aware." He tried again. "If they have left I was not aware. I am not aware they have . . ."

"I get the idea, Arthur," Delia said.

"They've ditched me," Crane said.

"Well, it's four o'clock."

The music stopped with a dum-titi-dum-dum on the piano; there was a crackle of applause; and the boys went out for an intermission. They went back to their table. Crane signaled the headwaiter.

"How much 's the bill for that table over there?"

"Mr March paid it, sir."

Delia Young's hand closed on Crane's wrist, hurt the bone. When the waiter had gone she said huskily, "What March is that?"

"Peter March."

"Richard's cousin?"

"Unhand me, madam."

"Richard's cousin?"

"Yes."

"Is he a friend of yours?"

"I don't think so."

This apparently satisfied her. She let his wrist go, took a drink of champagne. She poured some more in her glass.

"What do you do in your spare time?" he asked. "Work in a blacksmith shop?"

She said, "I'm tall." She seemed surprised.

"My wrist 'll never be the same."

"I feel as though my guts had been shot out," she said to nobody in particular. "I feel hollow inside."

Crane said, "I think the bone's broken." He gave his arm a tentative shake.

"Richard March," she said. "The only mug I ever loved."

Crane saw this was his opportunity to inquire further about Richard March. He said. "I'm tired of hearing about Richard March."

Her eyes were angry. "You don't think he'd look at me, Arthur?" She took hold of his wrist again. "You think *I* was the one who wrote letters? I'll show you. Come on."

"Where?"

"Up to my apartment."

"What 'll people think?"

"Listen . . ." She scowled at him, then laughed. "You're going to be the first guy I've had to *drag* upstairs."

Crane said, "I'll come quietly, madam."

He followed her through a door behind the magenta

curtain, into a dim hall with a bare floor. Another door, with a red bulb burning over it, and a flight of wooden stairs were at the end of the hall. Two Negroes from the band were smoking reefers under the light. Their eyes showed yellow-white as Delia passed. A man lurked by the stairs.

"Hello, Lefty," Delia said.

He blocked her way. "What d'you think you're doing, Dee?"

The voice was the unearthly, metallic, whistling voice of the burglar. Crane kept in the pit of shadow beside the stairs.

Delia said, "You came back, did you?"

"Just in time, too," Lefty said.

She started to push past him, but he caught her arm. "What's Slats going to say?" he croaked.

"I don't give a damn."

"Yes, you do." His voice sounded like voices of persons supposed to be making telephone calls in plays on the radio. "You're not going upstairs with anybody."

"No?"

"No."

She hit him. It was a fine punch, right on the neck, right on the Adam's apple. Lefty's head flew back, he caught the banister with his right hand. She moved up a step and hit him again. He fell down.

"Come on," she said.

Crane bent over Lefty. He was on his back, face to the red bulb, one arm twisted under him. He looked at Crane through wide-open eyes, but he didn't move. His neck looked curiously bent; blood trickled from his mouth.

One of the Negroes said, "*Wham!*"

The other corrected him. "*Wham!* And *Wham!*"

"Are you coming?" Delia Young asked.

Chapter IX

There was green carpet on the upstairs hall floor. There were many doors. There was a stink of incense and cheap perfume. Delia Young entered the next-to-last room on the right without glancing back to see if Crane was following.

"Close the door," she said over her shoulder.

The room obviously had been furnished by a department store. It looked like display window No. 3; Moderne, in green. There was a low davenport finished in a material that looked like green-stained burlap, and on it were three tan-and-absinthe pillows. The pale rug on the floor was about the shade of creamed spinach. Two white lacquered chairs had seats covered with the green-stained burlap, if that was what it was.

Delia had gone into an inside room. Beside a bookcase filled with novels in bright wrappers was a white cabinet. He found a bottle of whisky, some seltzer and two glasses in it. He poured himself a drink.

Delia called, "Mix me one, too."

He did, then sat on the davenport. He was worried

about Lefty's neck. He wondered if it had had a steel tube in it, perhaps because of a bullet wound, and if Delia's fist could have jolted the tube. Then Lefty would probably choke to death. He wondered if Delia had purposely hit the man's neck. He didn't feel so good about Delia. He took a drink of the whisky.

He had almost finished the glass when she appeared. She was wearing pajamas. They were of silk, entirely black except for a DY woven in white thread over her left breast. She had put on a diamond bracelet.

She got her glass and sat down beside him on the davenport, touching his thigh with her elbow. She smelled of chypre. Her eyes were underlined with violet mascara.

"I like you, Arthur," she said.

"I certainly hope so. I'd hate to have you punch me."

"Lefty had it coming to him."

"But won't he tell Slats?"

"No. That monkey's been trying to promote me for months. He knows what *I'd* tell Slats if he crossed me."

When she bent toward him a slit appeared between two of the buttons on her pajama coat, and he could see her white stomach. A woman was laughing shrilly down the hall. She finished the whisky.

"Want a real rear?" she inquired.

"Laudanum?"

"Yeah. A dash with the next whisky."

"I'm tall now."

"I didn't think you'd be yellow, Arthur."

"All right."

She patted his thigh and went to the cabinet. Some-one knocked and Crane started to get up. "No," she said. She went to the door, opened it a crack. A man's voice said something in a whisper.

"Like hell," Delia Young said.

The man whispered again.

"Screw, Frog." Delia slammed the door. "Frenchy Duval don't think you ought to be up here."

"Maybe he's right."

"I'm of age, ain't I?"

This was obvious, particularly as one of the two buttons permitting a partial view of her stomach had become unfastened. She came over and gave him a glass. "Try this, Arthur."

He did, and it was terrible. It tasted like cough medicine; it tasted like embalming fluid. It was really awful. He drained the glass.

"Not bad," he said.

Her purple eyes were surprised. "Say, Arthur, you can handle it."

"Sure," he said. "Can't your boy chum?"

"Who?"

"Slats."

"That mick!" She laughed, slapped his thigh. "He don't drink nothing but bubbles, and very little of them He's a businessman."

"I hear he's tough, though."

"I don't know." Her eyes were contemptuous. "He took a beating from old Simeon March without putting up a fight."

Crane was interested. "How?" he asked.

Delia told him. It happened six years back, she said, when Slats was trying to go straight. He got the state distribution agency for both March products, washing machines and refrigerators, when the man who had it retired, and was doing well until Simeon March heard he'd done time and kicked him out.

"He took it with his tail between his legs," she said. "He just quit trying to be straight."

Crane asked, "What had he been in jail for?"

"The alky business."

"He's been in since, hasn't he?"

She tasted her drink, made a face. "A year on an income-tax rap. He got out two summers ago."

Crane felt pleased. That fitted with the notes in

Richard's house. He wondered if Slats had known about Richard. That would have given him a double motive for the murder: Delia's betrayal and revenge on Simeon March.

"He didn't like the March family, then?" he asked tentatively.

"You don't know the half of it."

The half of it proved to be very interesting. After Donovan had been fired by Simeon he and Talmadge March and Dr Woodrin, Delia said, had decided to start a night club. Woodrin and Talmadge were to put up eight thousand dollars apiece, and Donovan was to manage it. Woodrin was in because he wanted to make money; Talmadge for the fun of being a night-club operator.

But it had been running only a week when John March found out Talmadge was a backer and told Simeon March, who made him drop out.

"They couldn't have a March in a business like that," Delia explained.

The withdrawal of Talmadge diminished the capital, and the club failed. Donovan was very bitter about it, Delia said. He finally got a gambler from Chicago to back him in another club and made a lot of money, but he still hated Simeon March. She said he was always talking about killing him.

This was pretty good, Crane thought. It pointed to Donovan, but it pointed even more to Talmadge March. He murdered Richard because of Alice March; John because he meddled in his business. And, of course, each death meant more money for Talmadge. And he was trying to implicate Carmel with the odor of gardenias.

"What happened to Woodrin?" he asked.

"He lost his dough, too. He was almost as sore as Slats."

No wonder Slats was angry, Crane thought. First Simeon March forced him out of legitimate business. And then John March broke up his night-club venture. And Richard March stole his girl, though perhaps he didn't know that.

"Does Slats hate all the Marchs?" he asked, trying to find out about Richard.

"Just Simeon."

"If he's so tough I'd think he'd get Simeon."

"He's not so tough, Arthur, I told you. He's soft inside, like marshmallow."

Someone knocked on the door. "Yeah?" Delia said. A man with a pale skin and a small black mustache opened the door. "Hello, Frenchy," Delia said. "Meet my friend, Arthur. Frenchy Duval."

Frenchy looked worried. "Look, Delia," he said, ignoring Crane. "This joint is just startin' to make money."

"So what?" Delia said.

"So we don't want any shootings. It'll give us a bad name."

"Who's going to do any shooting?"

"If Slats should . . ."

"He won't," Delia said.

"It'll ruin us if he comes, though," Frenchy said.

Delia laughed huskily. "You can't scare Arthur that way, Frenchy."

"Yes, he can," said Crane.

Delia ignored him. "Scram, Frenchy," she said.

Frenchy closed the door.

Crane said, "I think I'll be going."

"Yellow?"

"You bet."

He got up. In some way his glass had been filled with whisky. He dosed it with laudanum and downed the drink. "Good-by." The liquor hurt his throat.

Delia was looking at the empty glass. "Man! You drink just like Richard used to."

"Richard March?"

"Who'd you think?"

"You were never out with him?"

"You wouldn't want me to sap you, would you, Arthur?"

"No."

"Then don't get wise."

"I'm not wise. I just know Richard liked another girl."

"Yeah?"

"Yeah. Carmel March."

Delia Young's reaction to this was excellent. "Where'd you hear about her?"

"Oh, around."

"It was around, was it?" She drained her glass. "Gee! That's awful stuff." She tossed the glass into a corner of the room. The shattered pieces made a tinkling noise on the floor, and the dregs left a stain on the wall. "Well, let me tell you somethin' about her."

"Go ahead."

"Richard didn't go with her because he wanted to."

"No?"

"He was afraid of her."

Crane made what he hoped was a knowing leer. "Maybe that's what he told you."

"Maybe he did, Arthur. But he told the truth."

Crane had difficulty keeping her face in focus.

"I wanted to have her bumped for him, but he wouldn't go for that," Delia said. "I could of had it done in a minute. But he said he'd handle it."

"I guess he didn't, though."

"What do you mean?"

"Well, he's dead, isn't he?"

"Sure, but . . ." Her hand, just above his elbow, pinched his flesh. "Say! You're not tryin' to tell me she . . ."

"Somebody knocked him off."

For thirty seconds Delia was immobile and then, when she spoke, her voice was hardly more than a husky whisper. "How do you know?"

"Somebody hosed carbon monoxide into his car while he was in it."

Her hand hurt his arm. "Could she . . ."

"I don't know." He watched her face. "There was a smell of gardenias on his body. Her perfume."

Her eyes were wide and purple.

"Of course, Slats might have done it," he said.

She took her hand from his arm; scowled in thought. "It must be her. . . . Slat's would 've said something if . . . Say! How do you happen to know so much about this, Arthur?"

"I get around."

"I'm asking you a question," she said grimly.

Crane smiled at her.

"I'm going to have to sap you, wise guy."

Her eyes were coldly angry, but under the black silk pajamas her breast moved with her quick breathing. She drew a little away from him.

"I wouldn't," he said.

Suddenly her attention left him. She was listening to something. She smiled. "Okay," she said.

"That's fine." He started around her to the door. "Good-by."

Her attitude was strange. "Don't go away mad." She was smiling, but only with her mouth. She still seemed to be listening to something. "Have one more drink." She took hold of his arm.

"I have to go."

There was a noise of feet in the hall. Her face was suddenly savagely triumphant. She came close to Crane. "Darling," she said.

He was thinking, what the hell? when the door opened. "What's this?" said a man.

He was in a tuxedo and he looked like an ex-prize-fighter. He had wide shoulders, a barrel chest, a wasp waist. He was about six feet five and he weighed over two hundred pounds. He had blue-white eyes and a long pock-marked face.

"Slats!" Delia's voice was filled with terror.

The man walked into the room. Back of him came Frenchy Duval and Lefty and two other men. The man walked up to Delia, pulled her away from Crane. He turned toward Crane.

Delia pushed herself between them. "Don't kill him, Slats," she cried. "Don't, please."

It was an act. Crane knew it was an act. It was a beautiful act. But what was it about?

Slats pulled Delia away again. She fought him. In the scuffle Slats hit Crane hard in the face with his elbow.

"I wouldn't do that," Crane said.

Slats swung his shoulders, sent Delia onto the davenport. At the same time his elbow caught Crane's face again. He said to Delia, "Two-time me, will you?"

Crane hit him below his right ear, at the junction of neck and jawbone. Pain shot through his hand and he knew he had broken a knuckle. Slats Donovan looked at him with surprise, as though he hadn't seen him before. The blow hadn't even jarred him.

One of the men had gold teeth. He asked, "Should we bump him, Slats?" He was the bartender from downstairs.

Slats hunched his shoulders, and Crane got ready to duck. Then Slats said, "Hell, I just had a manicure." He jerked his head at the others. "Keep him. . . . I may want to talk to him." He picked up Delia Young and carried her into the other room.

The four men advanced on Crane. The man with the gold teeth had a pistol. Crane said, "Never mind. I'll go with you."

"Sure you will, pal," said the man. "Sure you will."

CHAPTER X

THE ROOM HAD nothing in it but a double bed. There were bars on the window and the door was locked. The floor was bare and there was only one light, on the ceiling. Crane sat on the bed and sucked his knuckles. He wondered what was going to happen next.

He didn't understand about Delia. The singer didn't care about him; why had she brought him to her room? Why had she called him "darling" when Slats appeared? Was she trying to get him shot because of his interest in Richard? Did she think in that way she could keep a secret of her affair with Richard?

Of course, Slats wouldn't dare shoot him. That was too cold blooded. But he was in a bad spot, anyway. Slats might beat him up, or have him beaten. That wouldn't be so good. He felt a little frightened. He wished he had a gun.

The door opened and two of the men came into the room. One of them was the bartender with the gold teeth. "How do you feel, pal?" he asked.

"I'd like a drink of water."

"Sure, pal."

He went away. The other man was younger. He had slick black hair and a green suit. "Can we do something else for you, pal?"

"Could I have a cigarette?"

"Anything you say, pal."

He gave Crane a cigarette. He lit a match and held it for Crane. The bartender returned with a glass of water. He gave it to Crane. They both watched him drink.

"You feel all right?" the young man in green asked.

"I guess so," Crane said.

"That's fine, pal," the bartender said.

"Yeah, most of 'em don't," the other said.

"Can we do anything else?" the bartender asked.

"I don't think so."

"Anything you say, pal," the man in green said.

They went out. Crane felt scared. If they had cuffed him around a little he wouldn't be scared. But they were nice to him. That was unnatural. That was what scared him. Of course, Slats wouldn't dare shoot him.

He had no watch but he knew it was very late. There wasn't any sound of music. The Crimson Cat was quiet. Everyone had gone. It wouldn't be any use calling for help. He looked around the room. The window was the only way out, but it would be necessary to break the glass to get at the bars. That would warn the guards. There wasn't a chance of escaping. He got off the bed and knocked on the door and went back to the bed.

The bartender opened the door.

"When can I see Slats?" Crane asked him.

"Soon enough."

"I'd like to see him now."

"Pal, you don't know what you're saying."

The young man was in the doorway. "Don't you like the cigarette?"

"Sure. But . . ."

The young man said, "Pal, you want to make the most of that cigarette."

Crane sat on the bed for perhaps ten minutes. Somewhere down the hall a woman was sobbing. He wondered if it was Delia Young. He regretted having ever seen her. He nursed his broken knuckle and wished he had a pistol. He was badly frightened.

Slats Donovan came into the room with the two men. The men looked very solemn. "Scram," Slats told them.

They went out and Slats sat across the bed from Crane. "Let's talk."

"About what?"

"About what you were doing with my girl."

"I was talking with her."

Donovan's manner was very solemn. "Delia says you had something else in mind."

"If that's her story I'm stuck with it."

"That's no lie," Donovan said seriously.

"What if I did have something else in mind?" Crane asked.

"I'd have to kill you."

The gambler was serious. He was really thinking of having him murdered, but he wanted to be sure it was the right thing to do. He was like a judge, stern and implacable, but fair. No appeal to his emotions would be any good. He just wanted the truth. It was different from anything Crane had ever encountered. He felt helpless and scared.

"The truth is——" He had to stop to moisten his lips. His mouth was dry with terror. "I wanted to ask Delia about Richard March."

Donovan had a long, lantern-jawed face. The rough skin was so deeply pock-marked it almost looked as if he had encountered a burst of shrapnel. But the remarkable feature was his eyes. They were the blue-white of watered milk. They were like the glass eyes of a cheap doll. They watched Crane without blinking at all.

"Delia did say you told her Richard March was murdered," he said.

"Yes. Somebody hosed carbon monoxide in his car."

"How do you know that?"

Crane didn't answer.

"Why were you asking Delia about Richard March?"

"Why don't you ask her?"

"Boys!" Slats called.

The young man with the smooth skin and the bartender were waiting in the hall. Donovan spoke to the bartender.

"Pete, this gentleman won't talk."

"That's very bad," Pete said.

"Maybe you can persuade him."

The young man said, "You want us to exercise him a little, Slats?"

Pete said, "This one is mine."

The young man said, "But you just got to exercise Lefty."

"He don't count," Pete said. "Lefty don't count."

Slats said, "Hurry up, boys." He found a cigar in his pocket, cut off the end with a pearl penknife.

"Come on, pal," Pete said to Crane. "Stand up, pal."

"Never mind," Crane said. "I'll tell you about it."

"All right, boys," Donovan said. "Scram."

Crane told him of his job with March & Company and how he had moved into Richard March's house. He described Lefty's theft of the letters.

"That aroused my curiosity," he said. "So I put the torn letters together."

He went on to his discovery of the house on February Lane and to his pursuit of Delia and Lefty. He said their anxiety to evade him had made him suspicious, and lying, added that as a result he had examined Richard's car.

It was impossible to tell from Donovan's blue-and-white eyes whether he knew this was the truth or not. It was impossible to tell if he had known of Delia's affair with Richard, or if he had just learned of it and was angry about it.

Crane went on with the lie. "I found a hose had been fastened to the car's exhaust pipe. That meant Richard was murdered."

Donovan said, "I don't get it."

"The hose is run into the car with the windows closed. The driver doesn't see it; he starts the motor, and in a couple of minutes he's dead. You see, the gas is odorless."

"That's clever." Donovan's long face was thoughtful. "I might have thought of that myself." He suddenly looked at Crane. "You didn't think I did it, did you?"

"I thought maybe you were angry because Richard pursued Delia while you were in . . . away that year."

"In jail," Donovan said. "A year in jail." The cigar had crumpled in his hand. He looked with surprise at the mass of tobacco, then dropped it on the floor. "I didn't know about the house in Brookfield," he said. "But I wouldn't have killed Richard that way."

"I wasn't sure."

"You are now, though."

"Oh yes," Crane said. "But having Lefty shoot at me, and then learning he was Delia's bodyguard, I naturally . . ."

"Lefty won't shoot at you again," Donovan said.

"That's fine."

Donovan's milky eyes studied Crane. "It's a smart idea, to use carbon-monoxide gas. It would pass as an accident in most cases, wouldn't it?"

"It certainly did in Richard's case."

"In fact, you're the only one in Marchton who realizes his death was not accidental."

"Yes."

"That's very fortunate . . . for me."

"How do you mean?"

"You aren't going to talk about it."

"Why not?"

Donovan's pale eyes were on Crane's face. "In ten minutes you won't be talking to anybody." His face was grim.

"You're joking," Crane said.

"You think so?"

There was a noise in the hall. The door opened and Frenchy Duval came in the room. He had his hands in the air. Back of him came Williams, holding a revolver against Duval's neck. Pete and the smooth-faced young man followed with drawn automatics, and behind them walked Ann Fortune.

"Bill!" she said when she saw Crane. "Are you all right?"

"Sure."

Williams spoke to the smooth-faced man. "You shoot, punk, and this gun 'll go off, too." He said to Donovan, "You wouldn't want the Frog's brains all over your floor, would you?"

The smooth-faced young man's face was undecided.

"What do you say, Slats?"

Donovan said, "Put the rods away." His face was impassive.

The two men put their pistols in their pockets, but Williams held his to Frenchy's neck. Ann Fortune went over to Crane.

"Are you really all right?"

"I'm fine."

Frenchy Duval's sallow face was the color of a turnip. He said, "I couldn't help it, Slats. This man, he caught me by the bar and . . ."

"Forget it," Donovan said. "We're all friends."

"Yeah?" said Williams.

Crane was glad to see Ann, mostly to be rescued, but also because it showed she wasn't too angry with him. "This is my little wife," he told Donovan.

Donovan said, "Pleased to meet you."

"I think it would be nice to go home," Ann said.

Crane walked with her to the door. "Good night," he said.

Frenchy Duval was frightened again. "Slats, don't let them kill me!" Under the pressure of Williams' revolver he walked stiff-legged to the door. "Slats!"

The smooth-faced young man had his pistol out again. "I can fog him easy, Slats," he said.

"Let them go," Donovan said.

Crane thought it was wonderful to be safe again.

In the hall he tried to take Ann's hand, but she wouldn't let him.

"Thanks for coming back," he said.

"It was Williams," she said. "I really didn't want to."

They were going down the stairs, and Crane could see the red light in the hall below. "Well, thank you, anyway."

Outside, Frenchy Duval pleaded, "Please don't kill me."

Williams said, "All right, Frog. Run."

Frenchy Duval ran away. They got in the limousine. "Where to?" asked Williams.

"Where's Richard's car?" Crane asked.

"In the Union Garage. They're holding it for the estate."

"Let's go there."

The sun came up on the way to Marchton. There were no cars on the road. When they halted for a stop sign they could hear a rooster crowing. A cold wind came from the east.

"What did Donovan want?" Ann asked.

"He was angry because I talked to Delia."

"What was he going to do about it?" Williams asked.

"I think he was going to kill me."

"Really?" Ann asked.

"I got that impression," Crane said. "I really did."

It was broad daylight when they reached the garage, persuaded the sleepy watchman to let them see the sedan. It was a big one, painted a cream yellow. "Plannin' to buy it?" the watchman asked.

"Yeah," Crane said. "Mind if we look it over?"

"Go right ahead." The watchman walked away. Crane examined the heater, found it was in perfect condition. Williams, peering over his shoulder, said, "No leak there."

"There has to be something," Crane said. "Or else I lied to Slats Donovan."

"Do you care?" Ann asked.

"I always hate to lie," Crane lied.

He knelt down by the rear bumper, ran his finger around the edge of the exhaust pipe. It was sticky. He held his finger to his nose, then stretched out his arm toward Ann. "Smell," he said.

"Rubber!"

"Sure." He led the way back to their car. "That proves Richard was murdered. The exhaust pipe got hot while the hose was on it, melted some of the rubber.

Now if we can find something wrong with John's car we can prove Carmel's suicide note was a fake."

Williams started the limousine. "We can bust into Carmel's garage. That's where John's car is."

By walking along the hedge which divided Richard's property from Carmel's, they approached the garage from the rear. Williams had no trouble finding a master key to fit the lock on a side door. There was a green convertible, a space for a car and a big sedan inside the garage.

"The big one's John's," Williams whispered.

Crane knelt and ran his fingers over the exhaust pipe. He smelled his finger, nodded his head, stood up.

"Rubber?" Ann asked.

Crane nodded solemnly and Williams whispered, "Then it's a double murder!"

CHAPTER XI

IT WAS PROBABLY the worst hang-over William Crane had ever had. It took him forty minutes to bathe and put on a gray chalk-striped suit. He tottered downstairs to the living room and found Williams and Ann talking in front of a bright wood fire. There was a tomato-juice pickup on the table.

"It's about time you got up," Ann said. "It's ten o'clock."

"Morning or evening?"

"Evening. You've been asleep fifteen hours."

Williams grinned at him. "You're sure you're alive?" he asked.

"You can tell I'm not a corpse," Crane said. "A corpse is livelier."

He carried the pickup to the blue couch and lay down with his head toward the flames so the light wouldn't get in his eyes. He pushed a satin pillow under his head.

Williams said, "Ann was saying that night-club gal, Dolly, mistook Peter for John March."

"I guess they were a lot alike," Crane said. "Brothers often are."

"I wonder if their voices were alike," Williams said.

"I don't know." Crane got the pickup to his mouth, but the glass shook so it made a tinkling noise against his teeth. "Is it important?" Some of the red liquid ran down his chin.

"Maybe," Williams said mysteriously. "Can you get Peter over here sometime tonight? I'd like to have that Jameson take a look at him."

Ann asked, "The Brookfield rental man?"

Williams nodded, and Crane said, "I'll get hold of Peter. He was coming over anyway." The edge of the glass banged so hard against his teeth he became alarmed. He didn't want to swallow a lot of broken glass.

"Do you want a straw?" Ann asked.

He shook his head. He put the glass down and took off his necktie.

"How do you figure John was killed?" Williams asked.

Crane fastened the tie around his neck in the manner of a sling. "I think somebody held him while he got the gas." He put his right arm through the sling and grasped the pickup.

The other two were torn between interest in what he was saying and what he was doing. "But how could anybody do that?" Ann asked.

Crane drew the tie away from his neck with his left hand until it pulled against his right wrist. "I figure the guy threw some kind of a hood over John's head so he couldn't yell, then wrapped him up in canvas or a fish net or something." He raised the glass to his lips, all the time keeping the tie taut with his left hand.

"What in the world are you doing?" Ann asked.

Williams was nodding. "Then the guy hosed the gas from the exhaust pipe to the hood."

Ann objected, "But why didn't he just hit John over the head and administer the gas while he was unconscious?"

Crane tilted his wrist and drank. The improvised sling kept his hand steady. "The murderer didn't want any bumps on John's head." He finished the pickup, let go the sling and put the glass down.

Williams said, "What's the difference? He might have gotten a bump falling down."

"No," said Crane. "Not if there was blood. A chemist could analyze the blood, find if the wound was made before or after gas had been breathed into the system."

"I see," Ann said. "The murderer wouldn't dare take the chance of an autopsy being made."

"Of course, this is just a theory, darling."

"Don't 'darling' me," Ann said. "Not in private."

Williams laughed and went out in the pantry for some scotch.

"You're still angry?" Crane asked.

Her voice was cold. "No."

"I'm glad. Because that dress is swell. It looks as though you were poured into it. You look . . . well, sinuous. And the color . . . just like the peppermints I used to eat when I was a kid."

She had to smile. "It's Schiaparelli's. She calls the color shocking pink."

"Darling, it doesn't shock me a bit."

Her voice didn't get any friendlier. "Bill, why aren't you doing something about these people?"

"I'm not well. I have a hang-over."

"That's all you do . . . drink and have hang-overs," she said. "I think it's terrible, with two Marchs dead and maybe more to come."

"Darling, there 're always dead people in a murder case."

"But these people . . . they're nice. Not like gangsters.

And it's so cold blooded! It scares me. . . . That strange gas strangling person after person while you . . ." She halted abruptly. "All right, smile."

"I'm not smiling."

Her green eyes were large and serious. "The murderer scares me, too. I dreamed last night I saw a horrible, pale man fastening a hose to the exhaust pipe of someone's sedan."

"Ann, you've seen too many movies."

"Just the same I'm scared. I feel danger all around us. And I can't understand why the Marchs aren't frightened, too."

"They do seem pretty calm. . . . I suppose because they think the deaths were accidents."

"*You* don't think they were accidents, but you're calm." Her chin was firm, her eyes narrow. "I think you're a slacker."

"But, my God, lady!" Crane said. "I have been working. You don't have to get yourself into a lather to do a little thinking."

"I suppose you have to get drunk to think, though?" She was really angry. "Or chase after women?"

Crane said mournfully, "I get my knuckles busted, nearly killed . . ."

Beulah came into the room. "They's waiting for you, Miss Ann."

Ann seized her black caracul coat, said angrily, "I wish my uncle had sent somebody beside a drunkard with me." She started toward the door.

"Where are you going?"

"To do some of the work you're supposed to do."

He watched her leave the room. Presently he heard the noise of a car leaving the front of the house. After a few more minutes Williams, wearing his black chauffeur's uniform, came into the living room with a bottle of whisky in his hand.

"Have a drink?" he asked.

Crane shook his head. "Where'd Ann go?"

Williams didn't know. He poured himself an entire glassful of scotch. "She got you upset?"

"No."

"Like hell!" Williams tossed off half the glass. "Waaah! Not bad stuff." He sat on a chair opposite Crane, put his feet on the polished table. "Well, I think she likes you all right."

"Sure," said Crane bitterly.

"After all, you did do a bit of chasing last night." Williams lit a cigarette, tossed the match under Crane's couch. "And she came back with me to get you. Not many dames would've done that."

"The hell with it," said Crane.

Discussing the case, they agreed Donovan had the best motive. He might have killed Richard because of his affair with Delia, and John March because he spoiled his first night-club venture. They both thought, though, he would have been far more likely, if he was murdering somebody, to have killed Simeon March, since the old man had frustrated his one attempt to enter legitimate business. Williams didn't think he would use gas, anyway.

"It's pretty subtle for a hoodlum," Crane agreed. "And he seemed damn interested in how the gas worked, as though it had never occurred to him before."

The telephone rang and Crane answered it. A husky voice said, "You like your wife?"

"My who?"

"Your wife, dope."

"Oh yes, my wife."

"If you want her around you'll scram back to New York."

Crane felt his skin tingle. "Why?"

"Never mind why, dope." The man sounded as though he was talking with a handkerchief in his mouth. "If you think I'm jokin' take a gander at your paper."

Williams hurried out and got a newspaper. He came

back very excited, tossed the paper on Crane's chest. The banner line read:

Gambler Taken For Ride

Below this was a picture of a thin young man with a felt hat pulled down over his eyes. The caption read: "Body found in Willow Creek identified as that of Charles ('Lefty') Dolan, local gambler."

"The guy at the bottom of the stairs," Williams said. "The guy with the hollow voice."

"Let's go," Crane said.

"Where?"

"To see if Slats bumped off Delia, too."

Ann smiled at Peter March across the champagne glasses, thinking he was probably the most presentable twenty million dollars she had ever seen. They were at the Crimson Cat again because of Alice March who simply *had* to see Delia Young.

"She's your husband's discovery, isn't she?" she'd asked Ann with innocently widened eyes. "I must see her."

With them were Talmadge March, who had come with Alice, and Carmel March and Dr Woodrin. It was almost midnight, and many people in the velvet-draped room were having late suppers. The tinkle of glass, of silver, mingled with blare of unmuted trumpets bearing down on the Tommy Dorsey arrangement of "The Song of India."

Ann's excuse for accepting a date with Peter March had been that Bill Crane was too ill to go out. She wasn't sure whether any of them believed this, or felt, as Alice March obviously did, that she was paying Crane back for deserting her for the night-club singer. She didn't really care; she wanted to listen to them talk, to see if she could detect a false note in their conversation. She felt it would be impossible for the murderer not to betray himself if one were only acute enough to catch the right remark.

Over the noise of the band, Alice March said, "That singer must be very, very attractive." She smiled sweetly at Ann.

Ann thought her pink face was the kind Italian painters used to float cherubs around. She would have liked to slap it hard. She said instead, "You'll see her in a minute."

A thin sound of flutes, a weird mumble of drums marked the end of "The Song of India." There was a muffled crash of cymbals; couples returned to their tables from the floor.

Carmel said, "Don't you wish you had some of her allure, Alice?"

For an instant Alice March looked like an angry Persian cat. She didn't reply, but Talmadge came to her rescue. "I've heard she uses the same fascinating gardenia perfume Carmel does," he drawled.

Ann wondered why he was trying so hard to establish the fact Carmel used a gardenia perfume. It certainly seemed as though he was trying to implicate Carmel in the deaths. It was certainly very suspicious.

Carmel said in a brittle voice, "Perhaps Alice should use gardenia. . . . Maybe she could keep her man."

"You're always trying to pick a quarrel, aren't you, dear?" Alice March said sweetly.

"Well, aren't you?"

"Why, Carmel!"

"Yes, you are. Only you don't dare bring it out in the open." Carmel's dark eyes glistened. "Why don't you say what you're thinking . . . you and Talmadge?"

Dr Woodrin said, "Carmel! Let's don't have any silly fights."

Peter March said, "Let's go home. I don't want to see that singer again."

"Oh, but I do," Alice March said, apparently undisturbed by Carmel's outburst.

Ann wondered, as the floor show started with a chorus routine, what Carmel had meant. What were Talmadge and Alice March thinking? She felt Carmel would like to slap Alice, too. There were certainly some dark undercurrents in the March family. She decided she didn't like either Talmadge or Alice. They both had an air of conspiracy about them.

She talked to Peter March during the floor show, noticing Carmel's eyes on them at intervals. She had a good time with Peter; he was fun. He was telling her about a bicycle trip he had taken in Italy. Dr Woodrin disappeared for a while and when he came back he sat beside Ann.

"May I speak to Mrs Crane a second?" he asked Peter.

"Why, sure."

Dr Woodrin spoke softly in her ear. "This is probably a joke, but while I was out that little chorus girl, Dolly, spoke to me in the hall. She asked me to tell you to leave, that you were in danger."

"In danger?" Ann felt her heart jump. "Are you sure she meant me? What kind of danger?"

"She wouldn't say."

"I'll have to talk to her," Ann said.

The floor show was ending, and she saw Dolly Wilson

in the chorus. The girl was very pale, and her eyes were frightened. She disappeared into the hall back of the orchestra.

Ann was getting up when Alice March said, "But where's the singer . . . Delia Young?"

Nobody knew. Ann said, "Excuse me a moment, please?" Alice said, "I'll go with you, dear." Ann said, "No, thanks."

Dolly Wilson was stepping into peach-colored panties when Ann found the dressing room. Her figure was like that of a boy, supple and thin, without hips and firm breasted. Her skin was good.

She said, wide eyed, "You shouldn't have come here."

Ann said, "You'd make a good débutante model."

She said, "Do you think so?" She blushed. "I'm not used to having women look at me," she explained.

"Have you ever thought of modeling?" Ann asked. "I think I could get you a job."

They talked, and when the other girls had gone Ann discovered Dolly had heard the bartender calling Mr Crane on Donovan's private wire. "He told Mr Crane you'd be in trouble if he didn't take you back to New York," she said.

She thought Donovan was angry at Mr Crane because of Delia Young.

"What happened to her?" Ann asked.

"She's all right. She's somewhere out in the country. I had a note from her." Dolly added with obvious pride, "She's my best friend."

"Is she with Donovan?"

"I don't know. The note didn't say. But Delia can take care of herself."

"Donovan likes her, doesn't he?"

"I think they're married," Dolly confided.

"But why did she let Bill—my husband—go up?"

"She may have liked him, but I'll bet she was using him to make Donovan jealous," Dolly said.

Ann wrote a note to Mrs Jacobson at Causeman-Mason's in New York. "She's the buyer there," she said, giving the note to Dolly. "I'm sure she can find work for you if you ever go to New York."

When she got to the table Bill Crane was there. She felt herself blushing. He had just arrived and Dr Woodrin was offering him a drink. He grinned at her and refused the drink.

"I'm on the wagon . . . for at least an hour," he explained.

Carmel March said, "You look as though you'd been run over by the wagon."

Ann could see she was pleased by Bill's arrival.

Bill turned to Ann. "Haven't I seen you before?"

"I'm your wife," Ann said.

"Isn't that a coincidence?" He was being very suave. "Or am I simply *de trop?*"

Carmel said, "Please stay."

Ann could see Peter March was very embarrassed. "I think it's time to be going," he said. He looked at Bill, then turned his eyes away. "Would you like to take your wife home?" He was obviously not looking at Ann.

"Darling, will you ride with me?" Bill asked.

"I guess I'll have to," Ann said.

"I thought I was going to stay in bed," Bill explained to Peter. "But I suddenly felt better. That's how I happened to come out here."

Ann saw the others believed only part of that. They thought he'd let her go out, then sneaked out himself to see Delia Young, not knowing Ann would be at the Crimson Cat.

"I'm glad you're not sick," Peter March said.

Bill said, "Stop at my house on the way home for a drink." Ann remembered that Jameson, the real-estate man, would be at the house to look at Peter. She hoped he would accept.

He did. He was pleased to have relations pleasant. "I'd like to." He looked at the others. "That is, if . . ."

"You go," Dr Woodrin told Carmel. "I've got to get some sleep."

"We can't go," Alice March said, speaking for Talmadge. "I'm sorry you didn't find your Delia, Mr Crane."

"Oh, I'll find her," Bill said.

Ann slipped on her caracul coat and they said good night to the others. They found Williams in the bar. He was drinking scotch and soda. The bartender with the gold teeth scowled at Bill. "You here again, pal?" he said.

"Don't 'pal' me, pal," Bill said.

Williams said, "Donovan took it on the lam a minute after you got here, Bill." He took a long drink of the whisky. "Talmadge March tipped him off."

"The hell!" Ann saw Bill was surprised. "They're still friends, then."

Ann asked, "Did you come out here to find Delia?"

"Yeah. I think she's dead." He told her about Lefty and the phone call. "And I looked in Delia's room. It's been cleaned out."

She was shocked about Lefty. "The poor man with the funny voice!" She added, "But Delia's still alive." She told him Dolly had had a note from her. "She's all right."

"You're pretty smart," Bill said.

"Somebody has to be."

"All right. All right. But you'll get in trouble, going around alone. Don't forget that mysterious phone call."

"It's not a bit mysterious."

She had to smile at Bill's face when she told him she knew who made the call. She told him what Dolly had overheard. "Just come to me when you need any information," she concluded.

Williams was amused. "Looks like you met your master, Bill."

"Darned if it doesn't." Bill turned toward the bar. "That reminds me, I owe you some champagne, Ann." He spoke to the sullen bartender. "Two bottles, Pete."

The man got two bottles out of a cabinet. Ann protested, "But I only won one." The man put the bottles on the red-lacquered bar. "Fifteen bucks," he said.

Bill put some money on the bar. "I know, only one." He took the bottle by the neck, held it up to the light.

"Make up your mind, pal," the bartender said. "One or two?"

"Oh, two, by all means," Bill said. He tapped the bartender across on the head with the bottle. It wasn't a hard blow, but the neck broke. He handed Ann the other bottle. "Here, darling." The bartender had disappeared behind the bar.

Williams paused to look over the bar. "That's a dirty trick," he complained, "wasting good champagne like that."

They went to the car and started for home. Carmel and Dr Woodrin had left, but Peter's car was still there.

Bill sighed with satisfaction. "That guy 'll think twice before he calls up and threatens us again."

Ann said, "Could Talmadge March be working with Donovan?"

"I think only one guy is doing the murdering," Bill said. "You wouldn't take the chance of blackmail by having an accomplice."

Williams said, "Suppose I turn up Peter March."

"You'd have my thanks," Bill said.

Ann asked, "How could you do that?"

"It depends on Jameson," Williams said mysteriously.

Bill said, "I hope Jameson comes through."

"I think you're terrible," Ann said.

"I've got nothing special against Peter," Bill said. "I'd just like to hang him."

"No, it's me you're against. You're just trying to run Peter down because of me. I'm glad I'm not married to you."

"I'm not . . ."

Ann felt very angry. She interrupted him. "You're doing your best to embarrass me—letting everybody at the Crimson Cat see you were chasing that singer."

"Didn't you let everybody see you were chasing Peter March?"

They quarreled all the way home.

Chapter XII

WHILE WILLIAMS waited for Mr Jameson, the Brookfield real-estate man, in front of the house, Ann got ice and glasses from the pantry. Crane stretched out on the blue couch in the living room.

"This feels nice," he said.

Ann said, "Bill, why do we fight all the time?"

"I guess it's my drinking."

"It's partly."

"Maybe you just don't like me."

"But I do. I like you very much."

"Would you like me more if I gave up drinking?"

"Yes."

"Then I'll give it up."

"Just don't drink so terribly much."

"No, I won't drink at all. But you have to promise to like me."

She came to the couch and touched Crane's neck with her fingers. "You're nice," she said. "I'll like you."

Her fingers were cool and soft. He tried to take hold of her hand, but she moved away from the couch. She went to a chair across the room. "What about this case, Bill?" she asked.

They tried to agree on a major suspect, but they couldn't. They decided Talmadge March had the best motives: hatred and a desire for money, but Ann said she was sure Donovan had something to do with the deaths.

"I still think he and Talmadge might be working together," she said.

"And I still think the murderer would work alone," said Crane. "He wouldn't dare have an accomplice. Too much chance for blackmail."

Ann thought, in that case, she would just suspect Talmadge. He would naturally hate John for informing Simeon March he was in the night-club business.

So would Dr Woodrin, Crane said. Probably even more, because he had lost all his money in the venture. But Crane couldn't see why the doctor would kill Richard, unless he wanted Carmel.

"He likes her," Ann admitted.

"But Carmel likes Peter."

Ann's face became guarded. "He should kill Peter next, then."

"That doesn't make much sense, killing a lot of people to make a girl you hope to marry rich."

"How about Simeon March?" Ann asked.

"Why not?" Crane wished his head would stop aching. "Don't they always pin it on the person who calls in the detectives?"

"And Alice March?"

"I always suspect people I don't like."

"You ought to suspect Peter, then."

"Don't you know I'm crazy about Peter?"

"You mean Carmel, don't you?"

A cool voice from the door asked, "What about me?"

It was Carmel March. Her black velvet dress was pulled tight about her waist by a gold belt, but below her flat hips it flared out in a soft curve. She had on long black gloves, and there was a gold bracelet below the puffed sleeve of her dress.

"You'll excuse my not standing," Crane said. "I don't think I can."

"We were just talking over the party last night," Ann said. "Bill has had a relapse."

Carmel came slowly into the room. "I knew you were going to feel bad when I saw you drinking champagne with that woman."

Ann said, "He went on to laudanum."

Carmel said, "Goodness! Champagne and Laudanum?"

"Nothing like that," Crane said. "I wouldn't spoil good laudanum with champagne."

"How in the world did you get home?" Carmel asked.

"By American Express, I think."

Carmel had a nice husky laugh. "I'm upset about Alice March," she said. She sat beside Crane's knees on the couch.

"Why?"

"I want to know what to do about her." She moved her body so her thigh was against his hip. "I need your advice."

Ann said coldly, "I'll leave you two alone."

"Please don't." Carmel looked up at Ann. "I want your help, too." Her dark eyes, shaped like niggertoe nuts, were luminous. "I'm really scared. Alice has practically accused me of murder."

Ann said, "Oh, she couldn't have!"

Carmel said, "She hasn't come out with it. . . . She just hints." She paused for nearly a minute, then added, "But I'm afraid a lot of people think it's the truth."

"But why . . . ?" Ann began.

Carmel repeated the story she had told Crane of Richard's murder and John's subsequent suicide. She concluded in a low voice, "I tried not to let it happen. I liked Richard, but I didn't care for him. I really didn't."

Crane almost believed she was telling the truth, even though he knew John had been murdered. She might have been fooled by the murderer. The note might have been cleverly forged.

Ann said, "I suppose the odor of gardenias and the lipstick on Richard's face made Alice suspicious?"

"You shouldn't have kissed him," Crane said.

"But I didn't. He tried to kiss me and I struggled. That's how the lipstick got on him."

Crane asked, "What gave Richard the idea he could have an affair with you?"

"John didn't pay much attention to me. He was away a great deal, on business." Her big eyes were dark. "I think he looked on me as an amusing possession, an interesting pet."

"But why," Crane pursued, "did you want Richard's correspondence if you'd evaded his advances?"

"I'd written him a few notes. They might have been misinterpreted."

"Oh."

Ann said, "I think you were brave to conceal John's suicide."

Carmel said, "I'm not brave now." Her eyes stared at ripe-tomato coals in the fireplace. "I wanted to find out if you . . . if you thought I should tell the truth . . . to stop Alice from talking."

"I'd keep quiet for a while," Crane said. "Remember, the truth would probably kill Simeon March."

She nodded.

Ann asked, "How does Alice drop these things?"

"She and Talmadge are always talking about gardenias."

"Why don't you slap her face?" Ann asked.

"Oh, I couldn't do that!" Carmel's eyes widened.

Crane looked at Ann with surprise. She should know a lady would never slap another lady. What was she thinking of?

The doorbell rang. Ann said, "That must be Peter." She left them.

Carmel said, "She doesn't like me, does she?"

"Sure she does," Crane said.

She was silent, and he thought what a really beautiful woman she was. She was alabaster and pomegranate, like the babe in the Bible. He wondered what had been the matter with John, going away on business all the time.

Peter came in with Ann. His face was clean shaven

and freshly powdered. He still looked a little embarrassed, but not sullen. "Hello," he said.

Crane said, "How about a drink?"

"Sure."

Ann mixed brandy and soda, distributed the glasses. She gave Crane a glass of tomato juice, asked, "You can have some brandy, if you want it, darling."

"I love tomato juice."

His hand was not quite steady, and in bending toward the drink, his head came close to Carmel's shoulder. He smelled the scent of gardenias. He wished she would use some other perfume. It gave him a funny feeling. He finished the drink, saw the others looking at him.

"Just a mild case of jitters," he explained.

Ann said, "Beside you a man with the palsy would look like the Rock of Gibraltar."

Williams came into the room with the younger Mr Jameson. "Here's Mr Jameson, Mr Crane," he said formally. "His bill is twenty-five dollars."

Crane didn't know what Williams was doing; he didn't know what Jameson was charging for, but he handed out two tens and a five. Going to the door, the real-estate man spoke to Peter March.

"How are you, Mr March? Haven't seen you since that day in Brookfield."

"I'm fine, thanks," Peter said.

Williams followed Jameson out the door. Crane thought, what the hell! He began to see what Williams meant. "Huh?" he said.

"You're going shooting with us Sunday?" Peter asked.

"Sure."

"Somebody 'll call for you at six."

"Gosh! With the Country Club party tonight, I'd better get to bed."

"Not until you eat with me," Ann said.

Peter said, "If Bill's tired you can eat with me."

"I'm not tired," Crane said.

"Come over to my house, Peter," Carmel said. "Eat with me."

"No, thanks."

"What's the matter? Are you angry with me?" Carmel demanded.

Peter March finished his highball, stood up. "Thanks for the drink," he said to Ann.

"You think I'm a murderer, too?" Carmel asked.

"Carmel!" Peter's lips turned blue. "Let's keep family quarrels in the family."

Carmel pushed against Crane, stood up, too. "To hell with the family!" She was really angry. "Why don't you say what you're thinking?"

"All right." Anger brought Peter's heavy brows down over his eyes. "I'm thinking you didn't have to be so nasty to Alice."

"She practically called me a murderer!"

"That's no reason to start a brawl." He faced her. "The Marchs have always been gentlemen and . . . ladies."

Carmel came toward him with quick steps. "Do you call murder a gentlemanly accomplishment?"

"What do you mean?"

"Don't you know that John killed Richard?"

"Over you?" His eyes, his mouth were *O*'s of astonishment. He stared at Carmel. "I don't believe you."

Crane admired the melodrama. A woman telling her husband's brother that her husband murdered his cousin. He wondered if Ann had caught the additional implication of Jameson's surprising identification of Peter March. It would be strange, he thought, if she were in love with Peter and Williams turned him up for murder. He looked at Ann, but her green eyes were on Peter March.

Carmel spoke in a whisper. "John did kill Richard, though. And then he killed himself."

Belief and a trace of horror came into Peter's eyes. "It wasn't an accident?"

"He left a note saying he'd killed Richard. Paul Woodrin saw it."

Crane felt almost certain she was telling the truth. He was sure there had been a note. Dr Woodrin wouldn't lie about that. Of course, she could have written the note herself, showed it to the doctor, then destroyed it.

"But why didn't . . . ?" Peter began.

"I was afraid it would kill your father."

Peter collapsed in the big damask chair opposite the couch. "Poor John . . . " He looked up at Carmel. "You should have told me." He looked at Crane . . . suddenly became conscious of him. "But these people . . . how do . . . ?"

"I told them," Carmel said. "I knew they suspected something ever since the night you tried to get my letters for me." She was very pale, but emotion made her black eyes magnificent. "And I wanted disinterested advice . . . whether or not I should tell . . . Alice's hints . . . "

"What did you say?" Peter asked Crane.

"I told her to see if the gossip didn't blow over."

Peter nodded. He said, "Carmel, I want to talk with you."

She said, "All right."

They went to the door. "Good-by, and thank you," Carmel said.

"We haven't done anything," Ann said.

Back in the living room, Crane said, "Was something said about food?"

Ann said, "I think I believe Carmel."

Crane sat on the couch.

"Peter believed her," Ann said.

"You like Peter, don't you?"

"Yes, I do."

"How would you feel if I told you Doc Williams just slipped a noose over his neck?"

"Bill!" Her green eyes widened. "You're joking!"

Williams came in from the dining room. "Not much!" He had a scotch and soda in his hand. "Jameson certainly put Peter on the spot. It was Peter, not John, who asked about Richard's Brookfield house."

Ann objected, "But Jameson identified John's photograph."

Crane said, "Newspaper photographs are lousy."

"And John and Peter looked a lot alike," Williams said. "That's what gave me the idea of having Jameson see Peter in person." He was very proud of himself.

Ann's lips were scornful. "That doesn't make him a murderer."

Williams said, "The voices . . . They sounded alike, too."

Crane explained, "Peter, not John, suspected Richard was having an affair with Carmel. So Peter caught her parked with Richard in the car. Carmel thought it was John in the darkness because their voices sounded alike."

"And when Peter comes back to the party," Williams said, "Richard has had a whiff too much of gas."

Crane improvised, "And then John becomes suspicious of Peter . . . and gets killed, too."

"But the suicide note," Ann objected. "You can't get around the suicide note."

"Who'd know John's writing? Who could best forge the note?"

After a long time, Ann said, "Peter, I guess."

CHAPTER XIII

MISS KIRBY did not appear particularly surprised when Crane, at three-fifteen on Saturday, buzzed for her, and announced he was leaving.

"I lasted five minutes longer than last time," he informed her proudly.

This did not make the profound impression he expected. She said, "Yes sir."

He got his hat and the tan camel's-hair topcoat. "You might send up that piece of copy on my desk."

Miss Kirby picked up a large sheet of gloss paper, glanced at it nearsightedly through her spectacles and turned pale. "Oh, Mr Crane!" she exclaimed, holding it out to him.

At the top of the page was an ink drawing of a refrigerator, and in it was the body of a man, folded up in such a double-jointed manner that his knees crossed in back of his neck. Beneath the picture was the caption: DON'T BURY YOUR HUSBAND: FREEZE HIM IN YOUR RAPO-ARCTIC!

"I don't think that's the one I meant," Crane said.

Miss Kirby found another sheet. "This must be it."

"Does it say: 'Your Kitchen is Our Laboratory'?"

"Yes sir."

On the way out, Crane stopped in Simeon March's office.

Back of a gigantic desk, with tall windows behind him, the old man looked small and slightly frail. That is, until he growled at Crane, "Well, what have you been doing?" His voice sounded as virile as a tugboat captain's.

"We've been looking up one of Richard's girls."

"What's that going to get you? Everybody knows Richard had girls."

"We thought she might throw some light on the death."

"Waste of time." The old man's maple-sugar eyes glowed. "You know where to look."

His wrinkled, brown face resembled an angry Indian sachem's. Coming from behind, the light changed the wrinkles into dark lines, made him look as though he had fallen face first into a briar bush. The tan-and-brown spots on his skin looked like bruises.

"Get Carmel," he said.

Crane felt there must be an undisclosed reason for

his hatred of Carmel. He asked, "Why are you so sure she's the murderer, Mr March?"

"Look at her," the old man barked. "Wears clothes like . . . like a kept woman."

Crane switched to another angle. "Why do you think Carmel killed Richard?"

The old man regarded him so viciously for a moment that Crane thought he was enraged at the question. Then he said, "I suppose you'll have to know."

He growled out the story without taking the cigar from his mouth. He'd heard Carmel and Richard talking with suspicious intimacy at a party one night about four months before Richard's death. John had been going out of town on business a great deal, and he had assigned a company detective to watch Carmel during these periods.

"Richard, too?" Crane interrupted.

The old man shook his head. The detective had reported that Carmel spent a great deal of time with Richard, so the old man had gone to Carmel, he asserted, and told her he knew she was having an affair with Richard. He threatened to tell John unless she broke it off. She denied that she loved Richard, but he was adamant. "Never let me hear of your being alone with him, or I'll run you out of town," he had told her.

She had finally agreed not to see him any more.

Crane couldn't resist a question. "But why did she kill him?"

"He wouldn't give her up," Simeon March said, looking at Crane through shrewd eyes. "So she had to kill him."

"But then, when things were fixed up, why did she kill John?"

"She didn't love him, wanted to get rid of him." For an instant there was real pain in his deep-set eyes. "And she knew I'd stop a divorce."

Crane said, "That's a pretty elemental view. Carmel kills one man because she loves him, another because she doesn't."

Simeon March snarled, "I'm not paying you for philosophy. Just get Carmel." His cigar jerked with each word.

"You hate her, don't you?" Crane said.

"Wouldn't you hate the woman who killed your son?"

"If I was sure she had."

"I *am* sure." The old man was shouting now. "You get proof. That's what I want. Proof." He got to his feet, leaned over the huge desk until his face was a few feet from Crane's. "Anything else you want?"

Crane moved back a step. "Why isn't Talmadge March your lawyer?"

Simeon March blinked at him, then said, "Too young."

"Do you think he could be hard up?"

"No. He has plenty of money."

Crane felt relieved that the interview was over. He was glad he didn't work steady for the old buzzard. He went to the door, halted. "Have you told anybody you suspect Carmel?"

"Judge Dornbush, my lawyer, knows something about it."

"Would he talk?"

"Certainly not!" Jaw set, he scowled at Crane. "Why d'you want to know?"

"There 're some funny stories going around town."

"About Carmel?"

"Yes."

"Why, damn them!" Simeon March hit the desk, made the humidor rattle. "They wouldn't dare talk about a March!" He glowered at Crane. "Even if she is a murdering wench."

He let himself in the house with his key. Ann Fortune was in the blue-and-white living room. The crackling fire put rose tints in her tanned skin, darkened the green in her eyes. She was wearing a gray suit with a jacket trimmed in Persian lamb. Her hair was the color of cane syrup.

She placed a marker in her book. "Hello."

"Hello."

"You're home early."

He backed up to the fire. "I got lonesome."

"Really?"

"Really." The fire warmed his ankles, the backs of his knees. "It's swell to come home to you."

"Why, Bill!" Her voice was warm. "Thank you."

"I was worried about you being alone, too."

"Oh, I was all right." She smiled at him. "But I'm glad you worried."

"And then I wondered . . . "

"Yes, Bill."

"I wondered if you'd let me . . . have a martini."

"Why, you . . . " She threw the book at him. It missed him, went into the fire. "That's really why you came home."

"No. I was lonesome. But I wanted a cocktail, too."

"Remember your promise not to drink?"

"Can't I have one? Please?" He looked at her beseechingly. "I'm tired. I've had a hard day."

"I'm sick of hearing that," Ann said. "All you do night after night is come home tired, wanting to take off your shoes and drink martinis."

"I don't care about taking off my shoes," he said. "I just want some martinis."

"Am I supposed to slave all day over an ice-cold shaker?"

"I slave over an ice-cold ice box, don't I?"

She admitted that was true. "I'll let you have just one." She got bottles and a tray of hors d'oeuvres, put them on the end table by the couch. She mixed vermouth and gin in a ratio of one to three and one half added a drop of orange bitters and ice. She stirred with a long spoon, poured into a cocktail glass with an olive in the bottom. "Just one, now," she warned him.

Refreshed by the drink and some anchovies, he told her of his interview with Simeon March. "He's bound and determined to hang Carmel," he said.

Ann said, "I wonder what Mr March would say if he heard her side of the case."

"He wouldn't believe her."

Ann said, "If she kills anybody it'll be Alice March. I wouldn't be surprised if she took a sock at her someday."

"Oh no," Crane said. "She's too much of a lady."

"Anyway, I think Donovan's in this." Ann's voice was determined. "And I'm going to find out."

"It'd be better if you went back to New York instead of getting mixed up with a lot of gangsters."

"No."

Crane saw it was useless to argue with her. He admired her courage, and, anyway, he thought Donovan was bluffing. He was probably sore about Delia and wanted to scare him away so he couldn't make another pass at her. If you were really going to kidnap somebody you didn't warn them first. He turned the conversation to Peter March, pretended not to notice a sudden chill in Ann's attitude.

"He's a fine candidate for the noose," he said, not without satisfaction.

"I'd rather not discuss him," Ann said.

"It was clever of Williams to discover he looked like John," Crane continued.

She didn't say anything.

Crane said, "Of course, Talmadge is a good suspect, too." She didn't seem to be interested, but he went on, "He's always trying to pin the odor of gardenias on Carmel and he tipped off Donovan I was back at the Crimson Cat. The only trouble is I think only one person did the murders."

"You think Talmadge suspects you're a detective?"

"Nobody does," Crane said. "Least of all Simeon March."

"Then why did Talmadge warn Donovan?"

"Because of Delia. He didn't know she had gone. He wanted to tip off Donovan; he thought, from the gossip he'd heard, that I was chasing her."

"He was probably right," Ann said. "And I think you're missing the most important thing, not going after Slats Donovan."

"You'd better concentrate on Peter March, and stop worrying about me and Donovan."

"I'm going after him." Her face was determined. "I'm not afraid of him, even if you are."

"Don't tell me you've given Peter March up?"

She didn't answer.

"Or are you afraid he is guilty?" he taunted her. "Carmel's a fine motive. Peter killed Richard because Carmel loved him, and John because she was married to him."

After a time she said, "You're nasty. I try to help, and you make it seem as though I was out after Peter . . . or his money."

"He does have a lot of money, doesn't he?"

She said, "I think you're horrible." She walked out of the living room with quick, short steps.

CHAPTER XIV

IN A CORNER of the Country Club ballroom Crane found Ann talking to Alice and Talmadge March. "May I have this dance, madam?" he inquired. He hadn't seen her since dinner.

She was wearing an evening gown of black satin which clung tightly to her body and then, halfway to her knees, flared out to the floor. The black contrasted well with her taffy hair. She fitted very nicely in his arms. She smelled very nice, too. She smelled of English lavender.

"You're a swell dancer," he said.

The music was on the sweet side, with lots of muted brass in the orchestra. He saw Carmel and Peter on the floor. They danced as gracefully, as effortlessly as professional dancers, but neither of them seemed to be having a good time. Peter's black brows were drawn into a scowling V. He stared at Crane without recognition.

Crane asked, "What's wrong with the guy?"

"He quarreled with Talmadge," Ann said.

"What about?"

Ann didn't know. "I saw them just as it ended," she said. "They were both white with rage. I think, if they'd been alone, they'd have fought."

Crane frowned in thought. "That's a swell family, the March family. Simeon hates Carmel; Alice and Talmadge hate Carmel; Simeon hates Richard; Peter fights with Talmadge; Carmel almost betrays John with Richard; Peter likes . . ."

"Well, go on," Ann said.

He said, "I think you're the prettiest girl here."

The orchestra wasn't bad, even if it was a trifle corny. It played some of the old pieces Crane liked: "Sweet Sue," "Who," "Star Dust," "Three O'Clock in the Morning" and "Melancholy Baby."

It was nice dancing with Ann, even though she probably wished she were somewhere else. She danced beautifully.

After a time he said, "I'm sorry I've been so nasty about Peter. Maybe I won't have him hung after all."

"I don't think you can," she said.

"You do like him, don't you?"

"Yes."

The familiar pieces the orchestra was playing made him a little bit sad. He thought it was a good thing she liked Peter. He had plenty of dough and he was young. And Ann would be a swell wife. It 'd be tough on a gal like that (any gal, for that matter) to hook up with a detective who suffered from chronic hang-overs. He sighed. He felt a lot older than thirty-five.

"What's the matter?" Ann asked.

"I don't know." He evaded a man and a girl in a filmy violet dress, moved into a clear space by the wall. "Ann . . ."

"What?"

"Would it help any if I explained to Peter that we aren't married?"

"No."

"I mean that we're working together . . . nothing immoral."

She said, "I'm tired of hearing you talk about Peter."

"I'm sorry." The music paused and they stood facing each other. "Look, Ann. I think you're swell. I really haven't meant to hurt you, chasing Delia and drinking too much."

The music started again; it was an old-fashioned waltz. The noise of the violins was sad. The dancers were more graceful than they had been, moving in smooth arcs, like ice skaters.

"I wanted you to know. Anything you do is O.K."

He took her in her arms, began to waltz. "It's my fault we've been fighting. I'll try to be nicer."

"I'll try, too."

He swung her toward the center of the floor. "Look, let's pretend . . . since we have to work together . . . that we like each other. I mean, as far as our conversation."

"All right."

He grinned at her. "I'm nuts, but a detective doesn't have a hell of a lot of family life." Her body, scented with lavender, was slender, supple. "I'd like to see what it's like."

She didn't say anything. He felt a little ashamed of himself. A slick-haired youngster cut in on them. He said, "So long, Ann," and cut in on Alice March.

She said, "You don't drink, do you?"

"A medicinal drop now and then."

"I need a drink."

"Come to the taproom."

"No. I don't want a crowd."

"Lady, you know this place better than . . . "

She pressed his arm, said, "Meet me at the entrance to the Ladies' Locker Room," and left him.

Ann was getting a rush from the collegiate stag line, so he went down to the taproom. At the table in front of the open fire sat Judge Dornbush, the March &

Company attorney, Dr Woodrin, Simeon March and two other men. They were drinking brandy. In the light of the blazing logs, the judge's face was brick red; he looked like a regency three-bottle man.

They were talking about the duck shooting in the morning, assuring each other the cold weather would bring the birds down from Canada.

"We'll see you, won't we?" Dr Woodrin called to Crane.

Crane said, "Sure." He refused an invitation to have a drink.

He got a bottle of scotch, some seltzer, two glasses and a bowl of ice. He had promised Ann not to drink, but this was business. His feet echoed on the stone corridor leading to the locker rooms, and he tried to walk on his toes. He found a green screen on which there was a sign: Ladies' Locker. He leaned against the cement wall and waited. He waited five minutes, ten minutes, nearly fifteen minutes before Alice March appeared. Her canary-bird-colored hair was disarranged, her plump face was white. She looked ill.

"Let's go in here," she said.

"But my goodness! That's the Ladies' . . . "

"Nobody comes down here." She pushed him past the screen.

He was relieved to discover a small anteroom with wicker chairs and a magazine-covered table in front of the lockers. He could see white tile and shower curtains at the other end of the long room. He sat down so that his back was toward the white tile, mixed two drinks.

Alice March said, "Here's how," and emptied half her glass.

"Hey!" Crane said in alarm. "You'll get tight that way."

"I want to."

She wore a brown evening gown. Her eyes were pink from weeping; her nose was a trifle red. She finished her glass, handed it to Crane. She had good legs, but the rest of her body was too plump.

They finished a second drink, and a third. Crane began to feel philosophical. It must have turned very cold outside, he decided, because the small, square windows in the locker room were frosted. Or maybe there was frosted glass in them. In that case you couldn't be sure about the weather. It could have turned cold without his knowing it. He fixed two more drinks. He was surprised to see the bottle was only half full.

He asked Alice, "Why have you been weeping?"

"I haven't," she said.

"Yes, you have." He closed one eye and looked at her through the other. "Is it because of Talmadge?"

"What if it is?"

"He's a nice fellow."

"He's a rat."

"Why, I didn't know that." He opened both eyes. "I can hardly believe it. A real rodent?"

"You'd believe it if you knew what I know about him."

"What do you know about him?"

"I know he's trying to protect Carmel."

"Carmel?"

"Peter and Carmel. He knows something about them, but he won't tell."

"Is that why he had a quarrel with Peter?"

"Yes." She laughed bitterly. "He had a quarrel with me, too. I wanted him to tell what he knows about them."

Crane waited for her to continue.

"He told me to mind my business," she said.

"This seems to be Talmadge's night to fight."

Her voice suddenly softened. "It's his cold. He has a terrible cold."

"What does he know about Peter and Carmel?" Crane asked.

She shook her head. "He wouldn't tell me. I think

he threatened Peter with it tonight. They had such a quarrel. It must be about Carmel." Her plump hands trembled. "Peter's a fool. He ought to know she's out to destroy the March family."

Crane nodded wisely. A girl was singing with the orchestra in the ballroom. He hoped he would be able to remember what Alice was saying. He took a sip of whisky to clear his mind, leaned back in his chair and closed his eyes. He no longer felt embarrassed about being in the Ladies' Locker Room.

She continued in a voice harsh with passion. "You don't know it, but Richard March was in love with her. She made him love her; then she killed him."

His eyes popped open. "Killed him?"

"She was responsible." Defiantly, she finished her drink. "Oh, she didn't kill him herself. She hasn't the courage for that, but she was responsible." Her glass slid across the wicker table, was nearly deflected to the floor by a pile of golfing magazines. "Richard wasn't so bad, either."

"A lot of girls thought he was swell."

"Sure they did." Her words sounded like sobs. Crane realized she didn't care who she was talking to; she was simply having a good emotional blowoff. "Sure they did," she repeated. "Why not?"

"He had appeal, hey?"

"There wasn't a girl in town who didn't want him."

He nodded to show he understood.

"And then, when he did fall in love himself, he had to fall for her."

Crane said, "Don't tell me you still love him?"

"I don't know." Her eyes glowed. "I loved him like hell once. I would have done anything for that man."

This was the second time Crane had heard a woman say she loved Richard. Delia, and now Alice, who should hate him. He was beginning to have an acute admiration for Richard.

He asked, "But what about Talmadge?"

She thought for a moment. "I like him, but in a different way."

Crane closed his eyes again. He seemed to be able to hear better with them closed. He groped for his glass, found it, had a drink. The inside of his mouth was numb, he could hardly taste the whisky.

"Why do you think he ought to turn up Peter?"

"I'll tell you. He——" She hesitated for so long a time that, thinking she might have left the room, Crane opened his eyes. "I don't know why I'm saying all this."

"Hell!" He poured her a good shot of whisky. "It's just between us girls."

"I don't care, anyway." She reached for the glass. "Peter hasn't any claim on me."

"Peter?"

"Yes." She looked like an angry cat. "I think he killed Richard. I don't believe it was an accident."

"Peter?" He realized he had said this before, and asked, "Why?"

"Because of Carmel."

He felt very confused. He didn't think it was the liquor, either. "But what makes you think . . . ?"

"He was outside before Richard died." Her voice was spiteful. "We'd been dancing, and I noticed he was looking around for Carmel. John was dancing with Janice Squires. When Carmel had been gone for half an hour Peter suddenly left me on the floor and went outside."

She took a drink. Crane could hear the music upstairs. He wondered how long he'd been in the locker room.

Alice went on, "Then Carmel came back, looking scared. And in about ten minutes Peter came in. He was pale. I thought he was sick. Imagine! I was worried about him." She laughed. "Imagine! I asked him if he was sick."

"Maybe he was," Crane said. "Maybe he went out for air."

"No." Her lips were drawn into a thin smile. "He either saw . . . or *did* . . . something."

Crane suddenly became aware of someone in the room. He opened his eyes, saw a pair of silver slippers, a long row of big silver buttons, white shoulders. It was Carmel March. She had on a black evening gown with silver buttons up the middle. She apparently had been standing there for some time.

She came and stood over Alice. "You louse," she said. "You fat, troublesome louse!" Her voice was hard.

She bent over and slapped Alice's face from right to left. It sounded like a paper bag bursting.

She said, "I've been wanting to do that for a long time."

Alice looked frightened, but she came out of her chair in a hurry, her head shielded by her left arm. "You . . . " she said, taking a step in Carmel's direction. She clawed at Carmel's face, left parallel red slashes on her neck.

Carmel slapped her again, sent her back against the table. Both the whisky bottle and the seltzer siphon toppled, rolled across the table in unison, shattered on the floor.

Alice fumbled for a weapon on the surface of the

table, with both hands flung magazines in Carmel's face. She was sobbing, choking. She rushed at Carmel, grappled with her.

For five seconds they wrestled, their eyes white and mad, their red mouths distorted, their faces close. Above the sound of their breathing briefly rose the music of a waltz, sweet with violins. Then Alice's tangerine-colored nails flashed in the light, tore more flesh from Carmel's neck. A second downward, clawing stroke broke the skin on Carmel's shoulder, tore off one of the evening gown's straps, half her white brassière. She threw both arms around Carmel's neck, tried to wrestle her to the floor. Carmel bit her forearm to the bone.

Alice's scream tortured Crane's eardrums.

Freed from the encircling arms, Carmel hit out with her closed fist, moved up, hit again. Alice, caught off balance, fell back against the wall, slid to the floor, remained for an instant in a sitting position, then fell on her left side. Blood oozed from the bite in her arm.

Carmel stood over her, watching her. She looked frightened. "She isn't . . . ?" she began.

Crane said, "The Hays office would never pass you like that."

Without taking her eyes off Alice, Carmel pulled up

brassière and dress. "Look at her," she commanded. "See if she's dead."

"I hardly think so." Crane got up and bent over Alice. "No. She's breathing."

"Thank God!" Carmel sat in Alice's chair. "What a terrible thing!"

"I've paid ten dollars for a seat at worse fights."

"If I'd killed her . . . "

Feet sounded in the corridor. Dr Woodrin and Ann appeared at the locker-room door. "Did someone . . . " the doctor began, and then caught sight of Alice. "My God! What happened?"

"A little tussle," Crane said.

The doctor knelt beside Alice, felt her pulse. He straightened her body, said, "Get me a pillow." Ann got two damp towels from the shower room, and he wrapped these around the girl's head. In the medicine chest Ann found iodine and bandages for the arm.

Carmel, watching them, was so pale that Crane became alarmed. He thrust a glass in her hand. "Drink this."

"I'm all right," she said.

"What happened?" Ann asked.

"They got into sort of a discussion," Crane said.

Carmel said, "Alice was drunk."

Dr Woodrin, from the floor, glanced at her with inquiring eyes. "It doesn't make any difference, anyway." He looked to Crane. "There 'll be no scandal as long as we keep quiet."

"I was going to call the newspapers," Crane said. "But . . ."

Carmel interrupted him, "Will she be all right?"

"Sure." Dr Woodrin looked boyish with his close-cut black hair and pink-and-white cheeks. "I think it's alcohol rather than concussion."

Crane said, "You'd better look after Carmel's cuts."

Ann found some alcohol, and the doctor bathed the scratches.

Alice moaned and sat up. She looked at them with incurious eyes. "I don't feel well," she said.

Dr Woodrin helped her to her feet, held her with an arm around her waist when she swayed unsteadily. "You'd better lie down for five or ten minutes," he said. "I'll give you some ammonia."

"There are some cots by the showers," Carmel said.

The surgeon led Alice to the back of the locker room. Ann looked at Crane curiously. "How come you're not scarred up?"

"It was a private fight."

Carmel said, "Not private enough, though." She

turned her great eyes upon him. "You're not going to pay any attention . . . ?"

"She was tight," Crane said.

"Thanks," Carmel said.

Fairly sober again, Crane watched her admiringly. She had been accused of murder, adultery and a few other more or less destructive qualities; had finished a really first-class drag-out fight, yet her composure was perfect. That wasn't all that was perfect about her, either. It was too bad, he thought, that Alice hadn't lasted a little longer. She might have stripped Carmel naked.

Dr Woodrin came back. "She'll be all right now." He looked at the door. "Hello! Who's this?"

It was Williams. His button-bright black eyes were excited. "Mr Crane," he said.

"What is it?"

"Something outside I'd like to show you."

"What?"

"You better come. The doc, too."

Something in his tone brought them all on his heels. Crane walked beside Ann along the corridor leading to the service entrance.

She said, "Didn't I hear you say you weren't going to drink?"

"I didn't drink very much." He had an idea. "Anyway, it was business."

She didn't consider that a very good excuse. "I thought we were going to be nice to each other, too," she added.

"We are." He tried to take her arm, but she pulled away.

"Do you think leaving me alone for an hour to drink around with Carmel is being nice?"

"It was Alice."

"Do you have to call them by their first names?"

"You call Peter, Peter."

"That's different," she said angrily.

Outside, bitter air stung their nostrils, made their heads ache. The moon was nearly full: its light silver on the dew-coated grass. In the distance, clear in the tranquil air, violins mourned over a tango, "La Cumparsita."

"This way," Williams said.

They passed along a dark passageway formed by parked cars, walking now on cinders. Their shoes made a crunching noise. The faces of the two women were like jasmine blossoms in the moonlight. Crane pulled his dinner jacket over his chest. It was cold.

"Here," Williams said.

They halted a few feet from a black sedan. For a moment Crane was conscious of something very odd about the sedan, but he didn't know what it was. Then three things came to his attention: the motor was running; a gray mist, almost like steam, was floating from the right rear window; a man was huddled against the right front door, asleep in the seat next to the driver's.

He knew the man was not asleep.

He could not tell, afterward, how long they stood there, watching the wispy mist above the rear window. It was the color of pine smoke. It was like air from the lungs on a cold day. It diminished and expanded; it was like very sheer gray silk; it was like cigarette smoke rolling from an open mouth.

"I heard the motor," Williams said.

Crane jerked open the front door, helped Dr Woodrin lift out the body. He held his breath while his head was within the car. He stepped aside after they had placed the body on the cinders, allowed the doctor to kneel by the head.

Carmel's voice was out of tune. "Talmadge March!" she cried. Her voice made shivers run up and down Crane's back.

Even in the moonlight Crane could see Talmadge's

face was discolored. It looked purple, but he supposed in daylight it would be crimson. That was the usual color of carbon monoxide victims.

Dr Woodrin stood up. "We'd better send for the coroner." His voice was matter of fact.

Carmel said, "It's Talmadge's car—why isn't he in the driver's seat?"

"I don't know," Crane said.

With a last sigh of violins, "La Cumparsita" came to an end. The clubhouse filled with a hollow sound of handclapping. Carmel March's breath wheezed in her throat. Crane went over to the sedan, put his head inside, turned the ignition key. He sniffed cautiously.

Heavy, sweet, cloying, an odor of gardenias clogged his nostrils, made his heart pound with excitement.

CHAPTER XV

OUTSIDE, AT FIVE o'clock, it was soot dark. The alarm clock was making a noise like a long-distance ring on the telephone, and William Crane hastily turned it off. He put on brown corduroy trousers and a gray flannel shirt, conscious of a frosty wind nipping his ankles.

Downstairs, he found Williams frying eggs in the kitchen.

"Where's Ann?" Crane asked.

Williams handed him a note.

BILL,

I'll be back before noon. Have an idea.

ANN

"When 'd she go?" Crane demanded.

"I heard her leave about half an hour ago. It woke me up."

"I hope she doesn't get in a jam," Crane said.

The breakfast Williams cooked was swell. They ate five eggs apiece, using bread to sop up the yolk on the plates, and finished the entire pot of coffee.

Crane sighed contentedly, said, "Maybe they won't come with Talmadge dead."

Williams wiped his mouth with a checkered red-and-white dishcloth. "A thing like another death in the family isn't going to keep the Marchs from something important . . . such as duck shooting."

"They're still pretending the deaths are accidents," Crane said. "I don't understand it."

"Maybe they're scared not to."

Crane led the way into the front room. "I better look at Talmadge's exhaust pipe, make sure a hose was on it. I didn't want to appear too interested last night before everybody."

"I'll do it," Williams said.

"And see if you can get any dope at the Country Club. Find out where Doctor Woodrin was just before you found Talmadge."

"You think he's the guy?"

"I don't know. A doctor might think of something like gas."

"But what's his motive?" Williams wanted to know. "The only connection he's got with the Marchs is the Duck Club, which ain't worth anything and which he don't own, anyway."

"Maybe he's after Carmel." A horn blew outside.

"I'm going to watch him, anyway," Crane said. "So long." He paused at the door. "You might be trying to figure out why Talmadge wasn't in the driver's seat of his own car while I'm gone."

Peter March was outside, looking as though he hadn't slept. He said they would pick up Woodrin and then his father. "Judge Dornbush is driving out by himself," he added.

In response to their horn, Dr Woodrin stuck his head out the bedroom window of his apartment. "I'll be right down," he called. He had on a blue pajama top.

Five minutes later they were talking to Simeon March. He was just starting breakfast. "I'll drive out myself," he said. "You go too fast, anyway, Peter."

He didn't say anything about Talmadge's death. He didn't say anything to Crane, but he looked at him through his brown-sugar eyes and Crane knew he was fired. He knew it just as well as if he'd been sent a letter.

Peter said, "We'll see you out there, Dad," and they left.

Dr Woodrin drove. He drove very rapidly, but with great skill, and Crane remembered that he had once driven ambulances in the Oklahoma oil fields. Crane wondered what he would do when Simeon March really did fire him. It would be quite a disgrace. He wondered if Ann had found anything.

He asked Dr Woodrin if there would be an autopsy on Talmadge's body. The doctor didn't think so.

"Won't somebody talk to the police . . . or something?" Crane persisted.

A gusty wind kept pushing the sedan to the left. Clouds obscured the sun; gray light flooded the countryside; the trees, the fields, looked as though they were being seen through sun glasses. It was still cold.

"What could you tell them they don't already know?"

"Well . . . about the bodies smelling of gardenias."

Dr Woodrin smiled. "I'd like to see old Chief Auerbach's face when you tell of corpses smelling of gardenias. He'd have you locked up."

The club was a farmhouse set on a knoll among hardwood trees. Just before the sedan turned off the gravel road a sign said: COON LAKE—1 MILE. The country was rolling and quite heavily wooded, and the earth was a rich black.

A stocky man in blue overalls met them at the door. "Good an' cold, Doc," he said. His face was like raw hamburger from the wind.

Crane learned his name was Karl Johnson. He and his boys took care of the Duck Club under Dr Woodrin's orders. A black-and-tan hound kept at his heels. He led them into the house.

In the clubroom, the result of the removal of a partition between the dining room and parlor of the old March house, were big chairs and two leather couches. The floor was bright with Indian rugs. In an alcove near the back was a small bar, and Judge Dornbush, his face pink, was pouring himself a whisky.

Karl offered Crane a double-barreled .16, asking if it would be all right. He said, "Sure." Dr Woodrin got him some gloves from the locker room.

Karl announced shooting positions. "The doc and you, Mr Crane, will go to Coon Lake. I'll paddle you out to the blind." He assigned Judge Dornbush to Woods' Hole and Peter to Mallard Lane. "I'll send Mr March down when he comes," he told Peter.

Judge Dornbush had his gun in his hands. "Let's start," he said. "It's nearly seven." The gun had silver on it, and the butt was carved.

Halfway down the knoll, the judge and Peter, with two of Johnson's boys following them, turned to the right, went away on a winding path through a patch of hardwood trees.

Peter called, "Good luck."

"Thanks," Crane said.

Ahead, for miles, he could see woods and meadows and black patches of soil, and further a ridge similar to the one they were descending. Blue haze hung over the river valley; softened the reds and golds of the autumn leaves. Occasionally, a silver eye of water winked in the early sun.

"Lots of pools down there," Karl said. "Every spring the river fills 'em up."

Crane was surprised to find there was no marshland. The earth, even in the low places, was firm underfoot. It was very black and smelled of moldering leaves.

"Should be catfish in those pools," he said.

Karl shook his head. "The water gets oily. It kills 'em."

They came to a small lake. A shallow stream flowed like a tail from one end, gave it the shape of a tadpole. Grass grew near the shore and ten yards out there were weeds. The color of the water was strange; it was iridescent with blues and violets and greens.

Karl pulled a brown canoe from some bushes. Startled, three crows left a golden maple, flew off with protesting caws. The black-and-tan hound appeared from somewhere and tried to get in the canoe, but Karl drove him off with the paddle.

The wind was cold and gusty by the blind on the other side of Coon Lake. Karl steadied the canoe while they got out, handed them their shotguns and three boxes of shells.

"I'll go for Mr March." Karl shoved the canoe away with his paddle. "Be back as soon as he comes."

The blind was the most elaborate one Crane had ever seen, built of cement and lined with pine. There were two stools in it, and Crane discovered his head was just even with the reeds when he sat down. In front of the blind two dozen wooden decoys floated patiently.

Dr Woodrin glanced at his wrist watch. "Two minutes to seven."

Crane shoved two shells in his gun and looked around. In back, about half a mile away, rose the bridge, covered with trees ranging in color from squash-yellow to tomato-red. A gust of wind made him turn up his flannel shirt.

"We'll alternate shots," Dr Woodrin said. "You take the first one."

"At what?" Crane asked.

"There 'll be something coming in pretty soon."

They waited patiently for ten minutes. Crane was glad he had thought to put on wool socks. He heard two shots in rapid succession to the right.

"Peter March," Dr Woodrin said, and added quickly, "Look out!"

Two mallards, flying about two hundred feet in the air, came down the stream. They warily circled the lake, cocking bright black eyes at the decoys. They went down wind, then came slowly in for a landing. Crane stood up and nailed the drake.

The hen banked and started for the left, but the doctor caught her just as she appeared to be out of range. She tumbled head over heels into some reeds.

"Good shot," Crane said.

The doctor said, "Thanks," and put another shell in his gun.

There seemed to be plenty of wild fowl around. Crane could hear frequent shots from the right and an occasional double from further away. He assumed this was Judge Dornbush at Woods' Hole.

A flight of teal, coming hell for leather into the lake, startled him and he missed two shots. Dr Woodrin got one and missed his second. The teal were gone in a fraction of a second.

"They're like greased lightning," Crane said.

He did fairly well on further shooting, and in twenty minutes he had four mallards. Dr Woodrin had two teal and six mallards. They both had fired two shots at a flock of seven spoonbills without result.

Crane began to feel familiar with mallard and teal.

The mallard, he decided, was a smart guy. His eyes were always bright with suspicion, and more often than not he'd pass over a place that didn't look exactly right. He seemed to like the land, and often appeared from a cluster of trees.

The teal, on the other hand, had nothing on the ball but speed. He was prone to snap judgments, and would race for an inviting piece of water without any misgivings. He could clear out in a hurry, though, when the shooting began.

Five spoonbills appeared from the other side of the lake, circled overhead. Crane got ready to shoot. Two of the birds came down toward the decoys, but Crane held off, hoping all five would come in so Dr Woodrin would have a shot.

"Go ahead," Dr Woodrin said.

Crane brought down the first bird. Immediately after his shot, as the spoonbill tumbled toward the water, he heard a pinging noise and a sound like somebody driving a small nail with a hammer. Dr Woodrin, taking his time, got another bird.

Crane felt the hair rise on his neck. He felt alarmed about something, but he couldn't imagine what it was. He sat on his stool.

"Coming in fast," Dr Woodrin observed.

A moment later a good flock of teal slanted down at them. The doctor got one and Crane caught another with his second shot. He thought teal would be easier to hit if they were bigger. He heard the pinging noise and saw water spurt up almost directly in front of him. He blinked his eyes at the bubbles and sat down.

The doctor was seated, too. "That's my limit." He lit a cigarette. "Now you shoot."

Crane examined the wood on the front of the blind, found a hole near the top edge. It was a new hole, about large enough to admit his little finger. He got off his stool and sat on the floor of the blind.

"What's the matter?" Dr Woodrin asked.

"You better join me," Crane said.

"Why?"

"I think somebody's shooting at us."

The doctor obviously thought he'd gone crazy. Crane showed him the hole. The doctor stood up to look at it. Crane pulled him down on the stool. The pinging noise came a quarter second later.

"Hear that?" Crane asked.

"You're imagining things."

"But the hole!"

"An insect."

"Listen!" Crane took off his sweater, draped it over

the shotgun, put his hat on top. He held the gun above the blind. There was a ping, a tap. He lowered the gun, but he couldn't find a hole in either the hat or the sweater.

"He's a lousy shot," he said.

"My God!" Dr Woodrin got on the floor with Crane. "Why would anybody shoot at us? And where's the report of the gun?"

"A silencer."

"What 'll we do?"

"I stay right here," Crane said.

"What a hell of a trick!" The doctor's pink-and-white face was angry. "Do you think it's a madman?"

"I don't know."

"We can't lie here all day."

"I can," Crane said.

After several minutes of silence they heard two shots from the direction of Mallard Lane. A moment later there was a faint whistling noise in the air. Crane crouched as close to the bottom of the blind as he could. He wondered if the guy could be using shrapnel.

"A couple of teal," Dr Woodrin said.

"Oh," Crane relaxed a little. "What if he comes off the ridge and rushes us?"

"We could nail him with bird shot when he got close enough."

They both looked to see if their shotguns were loaded, then waited in silence. Some mallard had settled among the decoys. They made efforts to talk with the wooden lures, quacking interrogatively. One of the mallards was within ten feet of the blind.

Crane thought they'd have very little chance if the man did attack. He could pick them off from a tree on the shore, or he could come out in a boat. Crane didn't suppose a shotgun loaded with bird shot could stop a man at more than fifty feet.

He didn't feel good. It was not a pleasant feeling to know you were likely to get a bullet in any part of your body you exposed. It was not a pleasant feeling to be shot at anywhere, but it was particularly unpleasant to be trapped. He looked at his watch. It was seven thirty-five.

"Listen!" Dr Woodrin said. "I hear a boat."

The mallards had gone away. Wind shook the dry leaves of trees on shore. A shotgun boomed in the distance. Not far away there was a faint splashing noise.

Dr Woodrin had his mouth close to Crane's ear. "We'll both come up together. He'll get one of us, but the other 'll get him."

Crane nodded, flicked the safety catch off his gun.

He got to his feet, his knees under him so that he could rise in one motion. He felt a little sick to his stomach.

Water gurgled almost beside the blind. Dr Woodrin said, "Now!"

The old house in the country didn't look occupied. In the gray light of early morning it didn't look as though anybody had lived in it for a long time. It looked gaunt and lonely, and yet there was a sinister quality of silence about it, as though the house was waiting for something to happen, something abrupt and violent and tragic. Ann felt a little afraid, and she wondered what she ought to do. Was Delia Young asleep? Was she alone? Ann's watch read thirty-five minutes past seven. She had to do something soon.

She had found the house through Dolly Wilson. At first, when Ann woke her in the tiny third-floor room at Fourth and Elm, Dolly hadn't wanted to tell where Delia was. She was frightened. But Ann soothed her, assured her nothing was going to happen to Delia.

"I just want to ask her something," she said.

Dolly thought she wanted to ask about her husband. She thought it was too bad a fellow with as pretty a wife as Ann would go chasing after a dame like Delia. She told Ann where Delia was.

"Thanks," Ann said. "And don't forget there's a job for you in New York, Dolly." She hurried down to the limousine.

Now the problem was how to reach Delia in the house. Ann didn't dare to call her; it might arouse someone else. She pushed through some half-dead gooseberry bushes and went around to the back. Rusty tin cans, discarded kitchen utensils, rags, pieces of cardboard, littered the yard. Torn wire marked a coop that had once held chickens. The kitchen steps were warped and some of the planks were loose; she climbed gingerly and tried the door. It was fastened. She wished Bill Crane, incompetent as he was, was with her. She supposed he was having a fine time shooting ducks.

The thought made her angry. She'd find a way into the house to Delia Young and she'd ask her about Slats Donovan. She knew with the singer's help she could prove Donovan was the murderer. That would show Bill Crane!

Near the kitchen steps was an old-fashioned cellar entrance, with slanting doors. The wood on the doors was rotten and gray-brown with age; she was able to pry off the hasp with a piece of wood. It didn't make much noise, but she felt a nervous tension within her, as though someone was watching her. She looked at the house, but green shutters masked the windows.

It took all her strength to lift the long, right-hand cellar door. Oblique light bared moss-covered steps leading down under the house. She was terribly scared, but she made herself go down the steps. It was very dark in the cellar, very damp and chill. The air smelled a little bit like the bank of a river, earthy and green, but there was something in it that choked her, made it impossible for her to get a full breath. Gradually her eyes became used to darkness; she saw the dim outlines of wooden boxes, two carpenter's horses, a broken rocking chair, a shelf of mason jars.

Black and bulky, a crude flight of stairs rose mysteriously across the cellar. Walking on tiptoe, she made her way toward them. She could hear her heart pound, could feel blood in her ears. She couldn't catch her breath; the damp, earthy air made goose flesh rise on her body; she had trouble keeping her balance on her high-heeled shoes.

Something rustled. She halted, lost for an instant in terror, and the noise ceased. She took a single step. There was no noise. She took another step, then another, and another . . . Something soft squashed under her foot, uttered a faint sigh. She would have screamed, but her throat was stiff with terror. It felt as though she had crushed some plump, small animal. She was afraid to move her foot. Her fingers fumbled with a match; finally she got it lit and bent over.

She had stepped on a mushroom. The whole floor of the cellar was dotted with the tan hoods of mushrooms. Their white, dead-flesh stalks gleamed in the light of the match. It was like a grotesque stunted forest. The match flickered, and at the same moment something rustled behind her. She turned and saw, just as the match went out, a big rat watching her.

She went on across the cellar to the stairs. Twice mushrooms oozed horribly under a foot, but she didn't stop. She wanted terribly to get on those stairs. Darkness closed in on her at the far end of the cellar; she had to feel her way for fear of falling. Finally, with her left foot, she found the bottom step and started upward.

At the top she felt for the knob to the door, but her hands recoiled from spider webs. She lit a match, found the knob, blew out the match. The door opened with a faint squeak, and she peered into the kitchen.

Blue shades, heavy outside shutters made the room's furnishings obscure. Two paintless chairs and a table occupied the center of the kitchen. On the table were dishes and a metal pot over which swarmed flies. An iron hand pump stood at the end of a large sink. She opened the door a little further and stepped into the room. A plank creaked under her foot. Eggs had been eaten from two of the unwashed plates, and a spider had spun a web between one of them and the pot.

Ann thought the web meant no one had eaten in the kitchen for some time. She wondered if Delia had gone. The house did feel empty. It suddenly seemed to her that Delia was dead; that her body was lying somewhere in the house. She felt a terror even greater than before. The dirty kitchen, bathed in blue light, suddenly became as ominous as the cellar.

She took a deep breath and stepped forward and then screamed madly. Hands clutched her from behind, bruised her breasts, finally found her mouth. The hands were strong and smelled of tobacco. She struggled, trying to catch her breath, but she couldn't free herself. She couldn't get air. The blue room became dimmer and dimmer . . .

Chapter XVI

They stood up, flung their guns to their shoulders, but neither fired. Karl Johnson sat in the rear of the brown canoe, his paddle held by both hands. He looked startled, then amused.

"Trying to scare me?" he demanded.

"Scare you, hell!" Dr Woodrin said. "Somebody's been potting at us with a rifle."

Crane looked at the yellow-leaved ridge, but he could see nothing. "From up there," he said.

Karl was quickly convinced when they showed him the bullet hole in the blind. "Come on," he said. "I'll get my .30-.30."

They hurried back to the clubhouse. Peter was smoking in front of the fire. "You're slow," he said. "I've been through for ten minutes."

They told him about the shooting. They got rifles and went up on the ridge, and presently Karl discovered a pile of brown oak leaves. "Looks like somebody was lying here." He felt among the leaves. "Look."

It was a small brass shell. It was about the diameter of a .22 rifle shell, but it was longer.

"But that couldn't hurt anybody," Peter objected. "A .22 rifle!"

Crane took the shell in his hand. "Don't fool yourself," he said. "That's a .220 Swift. It's the highest velocity small rifle in the world. One of these 'll drop a moose in his tracks."

They stared at the small shell with respect.

"You didn't see anybody?" Crane asked Karl.

"No sir. I waited at the house for Mr March. And when he didn't come I came back to the lake."

Crane felt sudden suspicion of the caretaker's long wait. "Why didn't you telephone Mr March's house to see if he'd started?"

"No telephone anywhere out this way."

Further examination of the ground produced three more shells and a black hairpin. "A woman?" Peter asked incredulously.

"It sure looks like it," Karl said.

Crane took the hairpin and put it in his pocket. They decided to see if they could find where the assailant's car had been parked. Karl said he knew where a car could come in from the gravel road.

Walking behind the others, Crane tried to think. He

felt the attack had been directed at him. He thought it was a lucky thing the day had been windy; otherwise the sharpshooter, man or woman, would have nailed him. He wondered what Peter had done after he'd finished shooting.

"Look!" Karl said.

A car had left tracks on a narrow road down the other slope of the ridge. It had been parked behind some bushes and it had gone out as it had come in, from the gravel road two hundred yards away. Its tires were not of any brand Crane knew. The tread looked like that of the vacuum-cup tires popular years ago. It left a series of small craters on the soft earth.

Nobody said much on the way back to the clubhouse. Crane wondered if somebody had followed him out from Marchton. He regretted having slugged the bartender at the Crimson Cat.

They were almost down the lake side of the ridge when a green convertible with the top down turned into the club drive from the gravel road. Dust rose in clouds from the wheels. The car was too far from the club for them to recognize the driver.

Judge Dornbush met them at the door. He was smiling. "How'd you make out? I got a cinnamon teal."

They started to tell him about the attack when the

convertible came up, halted in a long skid. Carmel March, wearing the mink coat over a tan sweater and a brown tweed skirt, jumped out. "Peter," she called. "Peter!"

They watched her run toward them, having a hard time with her high-heeled shoes in the gravel. Her face was like soap.

"Dad!" she gasped. ". . . Overcome . . . gas . . ."

Peter asked, "Dead?"

"No," Carmel said. "Not yet . . ."

Carmel went back to town with Peter, and Dr Woodrin took Crane in her convertible. The doctor seemed very upset about Simeon March.

"He just couldn't have been gassed," he said.

"He was, though," Crane said.

"It isn't reasonable."

"There have been a lot of people gassed," Crane agreed.

"It couldn't have happened." Dr Woodrin swung the car around a curve in a long skid on the gravel. "It doesn't make sense."

He fell silent, his eyes on the winding road. Occasionally his lips moved, but Crane couldn't hear what he was saying. He seemed to be agitated. He looked ill, too.

Crane didn't understand why he should be so per-turbed about Simeon March. Why hadn't he displayed as much emotion when Talmadge was gassed? Of course, the possibility that all the March deaths were not accidental might have just occurred to him. Then he would be upset.

Dr Woodrin got out of the convertible at City Hospital. "I'll see what I can do," he said. "Will you take the car to Carmel's house?"

"Sure."

Crane halted at his house, set the emergency and stepped out into a bed of dahlias. Williams appeared, his eyes bright with curiosity.

Crane asked, "Where's Ann?"

"Not back yet." Williams eyed the convertible. "Where'd you get the job with the outside plumbing?"

"It's Carmel's," Crane said, leading the way into the house. He felt a little worried about Ann.

"How was the shooting?" Williams asked.

"Lousy," Crane said. "Nobody could hit me."

He got a decanter of scotch, poured himself a good drink. He told Williams about Simeon March and gave him a graphic account of the attack at the Duck Club. He was so moved by his tale that he had another drink.

"You certainly have a tough time with your suspects," Williams said, taking the decanter from Crane. "You pick Talmadge and he gets knocked off. You pick the doc and what does he do but fix it so you're his alibi for the attack on old man March."

"There 're still some more suspects," Crane said.

"Is the old man dead?" Williams asked.

"I don't know."

"Who was doing the shooting at you?"

"I don't know."

Williams disgustedly emptied the decanter into a glass. "You're making a hell of a fine record on this case."

Crane said, "Well, *I'm* still alive."

Over their drinks, Williams related what he had done during the morning. He had, in the first place, examined the exhaust pipe on Talmadge's car. There was rubber on it.

"It was sticky," he said. "It came off on my fingers."

But his most important discovery was made at the Country Club. Slats Donovan had been seen there by the head locker man about the time Talmadge had died.

Crane lowered his glass. "You're sure?"

"Positive. Thomas, that's the lockerman, used to get his stuff from Donovan during prohibition. He said

he spoke to Donovan outside the locker room, thought
he was waiting for a member."

"That puts Donovan right up there," Crane said.

Williams objected. "Only I can't see a gangster
knockin' off anybody with gas."

The doorbell rang and Beulah let in Peter March.
His face was pale and tired. Williams nodded to him
and left the room.

"Is he still alive?" Crane asked.

"Barely. He's at City Hospital."

"Dr Woodrin taking care of him?"

"He's helping Rutledge, the doctor they called first."

"How did it happen?"

"Like the others . . . carbon monoxide. He was found
in his garage."

"In the car?"

"No. He'd fallen beside it." Curiosity lifted his eyebrows a bit. "What makes you ask?"

"I was just wondering." Crane stared at him curiously. "Peter, do you mind if I ask you something?"

"Why, no."

"Did you find Carmel with Richard in his car that
night at the Country Club?"

The question was like a blow in Peter's face. His lips
became loose, his eyelids fell over his eyes. "How did
you know?"

Crane didn't reply.

"Carmel shouldn't have told," Peter said after a long while.

"Did you kill Richard?" Crane asked softly.

"My God! No!" His black eyes were startled. "He was killed by . . . You know that." His eyes became angry. "And if he weren't, why should I?"

"I don't know . . . maybe for Carmel." Crane watched his hands, his fluttering fingers. "You didn't tell Simeon March you killed all these people, did you?"

Peter's face was pale. "I don't know what you're talking about."

Crane went on: "Simeon March didn't fake this attack to provide you with an alibi, to throw suspicion off you, did he?"

"You must be crazy."

Crane himself couldn't see old man March doing a thing like that to protect Peter. He'd be more likely to turn his son over to the police. "Maybe I am crazy," he said. "I get funny ideas."

Some of the anger left Peter's face. "What makes you think Richard and John and Talmadge were murdered?"

"Three deaths in the same family by carbon monoxide are stretching it a bit."

"I don't mind telling you about Richard," Peter said. "I didn't do anything to be ashamed of."

He said he had noticed a growing intimacy between Carmel and Richard. He was alarmed about it for John. So when they both disappeared at the Country Club dance, he went out and found them in Richard's car. He'd told Carmel to go inside, intending to give Richard a good tongue lashing, but Richard promptly passed out. So he had gone back to the dance.

Crane asked, "Peter, did you ever tell John?"

"No."

"But didn't Carmel tell you she thought it was John, not you, who caught her in the car with Richard?"

"You mean John never came out there at all?"

"I don't think so."

"Then the suicide note was forged?"

"I think so."

"My God! Poor John . . . " He started for the door. "I'll have to talk to Judge Dornbush about this." He paused in the hall. "Give my regards to Ann."

"I will."

Williams appeared, and they had a drink.

"I'm scared about Ann," Crane said.

"Oh, she'll be back," Williams said. "It isn't noon yet."

Crane telephoned City Hospital to inquire about Simeon March. He asked for Dr Woodrin, but got Dr Rutledge. He told the doctor he was a city detective. In reply to Crane's questions, the doctor said there were no bruises on Simeon March's body. There were no signs of a struggle. It was obviously an accident.

"Will he recover consciousness?" Crane asked.

"If he lives."

"Will he?"

"It's a fifty-fifty chance."

Crane asked him if he knew where the clothes the millionaire was wearing were. They were in the next room. Crane asked him to smell them.

"Anything funny?" he asked when the doctor returned to the telephone.

"No."

"You can't smell an odor of gardenias?"

"No," Dr Rutledge said. "I can't smell anything."

Crane went back to the blue-and-white living room and told Williams what he had learned. Both were surprised that there was no odor of gardenias. Until it was time for lunch they discussed the case. Crane said they had to determine if there was rubber on the exhaust pipe of Simeon March's car. Williams persisted in . . .

"We got plenty of clues," Williams said.

That wasn't what Crane meant at all. What he wanted was the relevant clue. That was the way Scotland Yard always worked. The inspector always singled out the relevant clue and followed it up to the murderer.

"How 're you going to know when you got it?" Williams demanded.

"It has to be something that appeared in all the deaths."

"Gas," Williams said.

"No."

"Gardenias?"

"Simeon March didn't smell of gardenias."

"But he ain't dead, either."

Crane looked at him wide eyed. "Maybe you've got something there, Doc."

Williams said, "I wish we knew where Ann was."

Chapter XVII

ANN HAD BEEN GONE five hours, and now even Williams was terribly upset. With serious black eyes, he watched Crane walk a frustrated diamond-shaped figure on the blue-and-white Aubusson. They knew for certain Ann was in trouble. Unexpressed, but strong within them, was a fear she had been murdered. They had searched Marchton for her and now they were trying to think of something more to do.

They had entered the Crimson Cat together, had walked into the taproom. The barman's face was held together by gauze. He saw them, reached under the bar.

"No," Williams said, producing a revolver.

The bartender's hands rose; he looked as though he intended to chin himself on an imaginary bar above his head. "When Slats comes back to the city," he said, "he'll handle you guys."

"Too bad he ain't here now, pal," Williams said.

Crane asked, "Where is he, pal?"

"I don't know," the bartender said sullenly.

"Do you know where Dolly Wilson is?"

"What's that to you?"

Williams leaned over the bar, grasped a bottle of Canadian rye. "Do we have to open up your head again, pal?" he asked.

The bartender said, "She lives at Elm and Fourth, in a boardinghouse."

Perspiration made half-moons under the armholes of Mrs Grady's brown dress. "You just missed her, boys," she said. "She left for New York at one-thirty." She was a massive woman.

A blonde girl *had* talked to Dolly, Mrs Grady admitted. No, the blonde hadn't gone with her.

Miss Wilson had left no forwarding address, but she was going to write as soon as she was located in New York. She'd better, too, Mrs Grady added, because there was that little matter of nine dollars. Maybe the gentlemen . . . ?

On a sofa under a peach-colored quilt, Alice March was eating bonbons and reading a paper-backed French novel by somebody named Vercel. She didn't seem especially upset over Talmadge's death, or Simeon March's condition.

"Carmel and Peter just left for the hospital," she said. "Won't you sit down?"

Crane refused. "I just dropped in to see how you were."

He and Williams agreed it didn't seem likely she was holding Ann.

Gloom filled the interior of Simeon March's big garage. The German gardener showed them where the millionaire's body had been found on the cement floor beside the open left front door of his favorite sedan.

"He warms the engine and the gas comes," the gardener explained. "Then he falls the door out."

Crane thought this was possible. He found, as usual, rubber on the exhaust pipe. As they left the garage, he told Williams the hose could have been stuck through a back window, as it had been in Richard's and Talmadge's death.

Williams disagreed. "You'd smell the gas."

"Why didn't the others smell it?"

"Richard was drunk," Williams said. "And Talmadge had a bad cold."

This was something to think about.

Before returning home they dispatched a telegram to the agency in New York, suggesting Dolly Wilson be met by an operative at the station and asked what she had told Ann.

And now Crane was wearing the diamond-shaped trail in the Aubusson.

"We can't call in the police," he said, "because it would tip off the murderer that we're working on the case." He halted in the middle of a step. "And a big search would probably frighten the guy into killing her, if he hasn't . . . "

Williams said, "I don't like not doing anything."

Crane walked around the imaginary diamond. "Our agency 'd be the laughingstock of the world if we had to ask the police to find one of our operatives."

"That's better than having Ann dead."

"When she went to work she took her chances." He looked at Williams. "A detective takes the risk of being knocked off."

Williams said, "We ought to do something."

Crane walked twice around the diamond, then telephoned City Hospital and found there was no change in Simeon March's condition.

Williams said, "If he recovers the murderer 'll probably take another crack at him."

Crane's brown eyes narrowed; he stared at Williams.

"In fact, a smart murderer would find a way to crack him before he recovers," Williams said. "In case he should talk."

Crane said, "By God!" He telephoned the Marchton *Globe*, got the city editor on the wire. "This is Doctor Amos Crane of Chicago," he lied. "I have some news for you."

"What is it?"

"I have just completed an examination of Simeon March—my special field is gas poisoning—and I am confident he will recover. He should be conscious by morning."

"That's great!" The city editor was excited. "What hospital are you connected with, Doctor Crane?"

"The Presbyterian," Crane lied. "But I shouldn't like to be quoted. Ethics, you know. In fact, I wish you wouldn't mention my call to the local physicians. I prefer to co-operate with the newspapers in an anonymous manner."

"Well, that's very decent of you, Doctor Crane. You'll tip us off if anything new develops?"

"I should be glad to. If you wish to reach me I am staying at the Richard March residence; with my cousin, William Crane. Good-by."

Crane felt pleased with this last invention. The fact

that he was staying at Richard March's house would put the seal of truth on his story in the eyes of the *Globe*. Moreover the newspaper could check back on him if it wanted to. And it would certainly preserve the anonymity of a good tipster. He got his hat and coat.

Williams had been watching him beetle eyed. "Where are you going?"

"To March & Company . . . to get some guards for the hospital."

"And then . . . ?"

"I'm going to sit up all night with Simeon March."

"I'll go with you."

"No." Crane walked to the door. "You sit here until the first edition of the *Globe* comes out. And remember, until then you're Doc Crane, the specialist from Chicago."

Chapter XVIII

ONLY THE NIGHT LAMP, a wan bulb with a meager supply of honey-pale electricity, provided illumination for the room. A circular puddle of light at the lamp's base showed a white table top, a glass half filled with water, a green thermos bottle. Gloom blurred the outlines of the room's other furniture, gave a fourth dimensional quality to Simeon March's bed, two chairs, a dresser. Cold air seeped through a half-open window.

Crane, on a chair back of the screen in the corner of the room, waited for the murderer.

He had been waiting for six hours and he was not happy. His neck ached from the rigidity with which he had held himself in his chair. He wanted a drink to quiet nerves that fluttered with every unusual sound. He wanted someone to talk to. He was worried like hell about Ann.

It was after midnight. Quiet, more nerve racking than the early evening bustle, had descended upon City Hospital. There were no calls for doctors over the loud-speaker system. Few used the corridors; occasionally a nurse would pass his door on tiptoe. At long intervals he could hear the whine of the elevator's electric motor.

Crane remembered how Ann had looked when he saw her last. She had looked trim and efficient, but her green eyes, her sawdust-colored hair, he thought, would certainly have got her into trouble if she had gone to the Crimson Cat. He, himself, had always admired tanned blondes; it wasn't every blonde—what was that? He held his breath. A small gust of wind rustled the curtains. He breathed again. What was he thinking of? Oh yes. Most blondes didn't tan well.

It had been necessary to tell Dr Rutledge and Dr Woodrin that he expected another attack on Simeon March. They had agreed to let him remain in the room, and had allowed him to place guards from the March Company plant at the front and back entrances to the hospital. Neither doctor treated this plan seriously, but the night nurse, Miss Edens, a pretty dark-haired girl, was impressed. She was spending the night in a small anteroom connected by a door to Simeon March's room.

Dr Rutledge had paid Crane visits at eight, ten and midnight. "Everything's ready," he whispered on his last appearance. "There are men at both back and front doors."

"I wish there was one under the bed," said Crane plaintively.

Grinning, Dr Rutledge said Dr Woodrin would take over at three. "If you're still alive."

A clock somewhere outside uttered a single gonglike note. He wondered if it was one, or half-past twelve. Or, hopefully, half-past one. The shade rustled again and his heart jumped. The elevator motor whined; there was a clashing noise as its metal door was opened and closed; heavy feet passed along the corridor. The wind was blowing stronger and the curtains, ghostly in the dim light, were dancing. There was an odor of chloroform in the air. A blue globe in the corridor threw a curious shadow on the ceiling by the transom. It looked like the shadow of a man wearing a cloak.

Somebody was bending over the bed. He clawed for his revolver under his arm, then saw it was the nurse.

"My God!" he said. "Don't scare me like that."

"You were asleep," she said.

"I couldn't have been."

Her voice was very small. "Do you want anything?"

"I'd like a drink."

"Dr Rutledge said he'd send you some whisky."

"He'd better bring a lot."

"Not so loud." Her voice was soft. "Do you want anything else?"

"No, just whisky."

There was a slight tapping at the door to the ante-room in which Miss Edens had a cot. She left him. The curtains beside the open window were almost parallel to the floor; the wind was cold and steady. A door slammed somewhere down the corridor.

Miss Edens came back. "The floor nurse with a paper," she said.

"What's it say?"

She tilted the lamp so the light reached the screen. In the saffron light they read:

SIMEON MARCH IS FOURTH VICTIM OF CARBON MONOXIDE

Simeon March, first citizen of Marchton, was recovering in City Hospital last night from severe carbon-monoxide poisoning. He was overcome early Sunday in the garage back of his home at 1703 Park Street.

He is the fourth member of the March family in less than a year to be the victim of accidental carbon-monoxide poisoning. The other three resulted fatally.

However, Mr March's chances of recovery, according to physicians at City Hospital, are good, owing to speedy injection of methylene blue, latest remedy for the deadly gas. It was said he might regain consciousness before morning.

The millionaire was discovered by Mrs Minnie Kruger, 55, of 904 E. Third Street, a cook in the March household. She said she became alarmed at her master's failure to emerge from the garage and had gone to . . .

The remainder of the story, running all over the front page of the paper, was mostly of the discovery of the body and an account of the millionaire's career. Crane felt a little better. The newspaper had fallen for his story, and the murderer would probably fall for it, too, and be worried by what Simeon March would say when he regained consciousness.

Only the important thing was: What had happened to Ann?

Miss Edens took the paper, put the lamp in place, touched his shoulder lightly and went into the anteroom. She was a nice girl, he thought.

The clock outside made a noise—bong bong—and it was two o'clock.

Still coming through the window, the wind at intervals made a sound like a frightened horse blowing out breath. It was very cold. One of the curtains was stuck to something, but the other performed a macabre dance. It smelled as though snow was on the way.

He thought of the dead men in the case. There had been a lot—too many! It was not a neat case. He liked murder cases where there was one corpse and no prospects of any more. Then the problem became academic, with no haste and plenty of time for drinking at the client's expense. But this one wasn't a murder case; it was a massacre.

The dead: Richard March, John March, Talmadge March, maybe Simeon March and Lefty—what was his name? And three out of the five dead from a silent, odorless, creeping gas that filled their lungs and turned their bodies pink. What was the link between them?

And then there was Ann. . . .

It was a really lousy case. He wondered what Colonel Black, his boss and Ann's uncle, would say to him. Especially since Ann was gone. He wondered where Williams was.

He was glad, though, the window was open. Suppose someone tried to pump carbon monoxide into the room. The idea was farfetched, but it made him shiver. He supposed it was perfectly possible to carry the gas in metal containers under pressure like oxygen. He wouldn't be able to detect its presence, unless he found himself getting drowsy. And he was drowsy!

In quick alarm he looked at the window. It was still open; both curtains were waving now. He decided he'd freeze rather than lower that window. Good old window.

There was something horrible about dying of gas. Maybe it was just dying that was horrible, but it didn't seem so bad to die by gun, or by knife, or by hanging. Possibly those deaths seemed natural because people for a long time had been dying in those ways. But this gas, without odor, without color, like voodoo magic, crept upon its victim, left him to meet, gasping and blushing, an unnatural death.

Ann's face, young and frightened, came to mind. He opened his eyes and stared at the curtains.

Simeon March began to moan. With each exhalation he moaned, making a sort of *aaaaaanaaahaa* with his breath. The moans seemed to come from deep within his body; his chest gave them a resonant quality. It sounded as though he moaned, listened for an answer that didn't come, then moaned again.

Miss Edens came quietly into the room.

"Are you all right?"

"That's not me."

"I know. I thought I'd see if you were all right."

"I'm fine."

"I'm going to lie down for a little while."

"All right."

After a minute the light in her room went off. He settled down further in his chair. It was getting very cold.

Simeon March was still moaning. In the corridor two nurses were whispering. Their hushed voices sounded foreign; so many *s*'s and *th*'s came to his ears. In the street someone was trying to start an automobile.

The engine was cold; it would catch, splutter, cough, then die.

It must be three, he thought; he must have missed two-thirty. As he was debating this the clock made a single bong. The minutes were moving like snails.

The next half-hour seemed a night. He moved around, but he couldn't find a really comfortable position. At intervals he reached under his arm to make sure his revolver was still there. He had a feeling someone was watching him, but he knew this was impossible. The automobile engine had finally started, and the automobile had gone away with a noisy meshing of cold gears. Simeon March still moaned. He wondered why someone didn't do something about him.

He wondered what could possibly have happened to Ann. He remembered the fun he'd had with her in New York. He remembered a walk in soft rain through Central Park on an April morning, the gift of a straw-enclosed bottle of chianti from a restaurant proprietor who thought they were newlyweds, watching Army play in the Polo Grounds with Ann sharing his fur rug, a mad swing session with Stuff Smith at the Onyx Club, a brief, surprised kiss in a taxicab. . . .

At last three o'clock came, but he didn't feel any better. He knew ahead of him lay another night until three-thirty, and another until four, and another until four-thirty. By five he'd probably be mad, if he wasn't already. He hoped Ann was having an easier time. He'd welcome the arrival of the murderer. Anything was better than waiting. Why the hell didn't they shut up Simeon March?

The elevator whined, but it didn't stop at his floor. Like the veils of a classical dancer, the curtains quivered in the wind. There was light enough in the room to see their movements, sometimes languid, sometimes wild. The blue light in the corridor gave them a milky, diaphanous appearance, but it was strange; they cast no shadows. He watched them closely during an angry tarantella, but there were no shadows. It was like ghosts dancing.

A man was standing beside the bed. He must have come through the door on rubber-soled shoes, have tiptoed to the bed. Noiselessly, he put a black bag on the table under the shadow; only his hands were visible.

Hardly breathing, Crane remained motionless.

In the lime-colored rays from the lamp the hands were an unhealthy white. Sparse black hair grew from the wrists to the knuckles, sprouted in tufts from the fingers. The fingers were strong and supple. They opened the black case and withdrew an atomizer with a metal snout and an egg-size rubber bulb. This they put on the table, then returned to the bag. Without haste, but quickly, they emerged with a silver hypodermic syringe.

The right hand held the syringe between the first two fingers. The thumb pressed the plunger a fraction of an inch and fluid bubbled from the needle, fell in two drops to the table.

"Aaaaaaaanaaahaa," moaned Simeon March.

The man in the room moved closer to the bed. He held the hypodermic syringe in his right hand; with his left hand he reached for Simeon March's arm.

"No!" Crane flung himself off the chair, jerked out the revolver. "I've got you covered! Don't move!"

Simultaneously, the lights flashed on. Crane aimed the revolver at the man. Miss Edens stood by the door, her left hand on the light switch.

Holding the hypodermic syringe, Dr Woodrin blinked at them, his pink-and-white face astonished and alarmed. "My God!" he exclaimed. "You gave me a start." He bent over Simeon March and gave him an injection with the syringe. "I thought you were both in the anteroom."

Crane said, "I thought it was better to wait in the same room."

"How is he, Doctor?" Miss Edens asked.

Dr Woodrin put the syringe and the atomizer in the black bag. "The next hour or two will tell. I think he'll live, but how the morning paper can be so sure is beyond me."

"Newspapers are that way," Crane said. "But maybe the murderer will believe them."

The white skin over the doctor's nose wrinkled in two V's when he thought. "If there is a murderer . . . You know I really think these deaths were accidental."

"Maybe you're right," Crane said. "We'll see. If there was a murderer he won't want Simeon March to recover, particularly if the old man saw him."

"That's reasonable enough." Dr Woodrin picked up the bag. "Good luck. If you need me I'll be downstairs with Peter and Carmel."

With the room dark, it didn't take Crane long to become thoroughly nervous again. The encounter with the doctor, although it was all right, hadn't been quieting. He shuddered when he thought of the weird effect made by the doctor's hands in the puddle of light from the night lamp. The effect was like that of those horror movies Universal used to make in which the hero is fastened to an operating table in a cathedral-size laboratory and a mad scientist gets ready to change him into an ape.

He decided he had never really appreciated the truth of those movies.

He had, he admitted, for a moment thought the doctor was planning to inject Simeon March with something to prevent his recovery. Yet the doctor, when the lights were on, had gone ahead with the injection. He wouldn't have dared kill the old man before witnesses. And besides, he was definitely not involved in the attempt upon Simeon March.

He was still thinking about the case when the clock outside struck four. He had a feeling the solution was within reach of his brain if only he could get the facts in their correct perspective. What was the thing he'd been talking about earlier that day? Oh yes, the relevant clue. The persistent odor of gardenias; how did they fit into the picture?

And Ann! What could he do about her?

He heard a faint noise in the corridor and held his breath. Somebody was whispering; a man said something, a woman replied, and then there was silence. Simeon March no longer moaned, but he was breathing hoarsely.

He thought about the attack at the Duck Club. Was it really on him? And if it was, why had it been made? He certainly had no information that would make it worth while for the murderer to kill him. Could the attack have been on Dr Woodrin?

The wind had suddenly died, and the curtains hung limply beside the half-open window. From a switch engine a long distance away came two shrill toots. The room felt as though it had been packed with ice. It felt like a cold-storage vault.

The nurse came in and stood beside Crane's bed.

"I'm afraid it's a flop," she said.

"There's still two hours."

"I fixed you a drink." She handed him a glass. "A Mr Williams sent it up."

"That was thoughtful of him."

The whisky, well diluted with water, was smooth. It warmed his throat, his stomach, made his mouth feel clean. He felt better immediately. She took the glass, returned to her room.

He felt a little sleepy. He was no longer scared; the whisky had fixed that, and there was only a mild feeling of excitement. He supposed that he had been over-ambitious in his plans for the murderer's capture; the murderer must have known about them. Yet who did know? He and Williams, Dr Rutledge and Dr Woodrin, and the nurse. That was all; not even the men guarding the hospital knew.

A dog two blocks away was barking at something. His barks came in bursts of threes, finishing up on an interrogative note, as though he wasn't sure what he was barking about. The queer blue shadow of a man with a cloak was still on the ceiling by the transom.

Crane twisted his body so he was sitting on his left hip and thought: to hell with it all! To hell with the blue man in the cloak! To hell with all the various and sundry noises! A hospital was the last place he'd ever go for a rest.

He wondered, suddenly feeling sick to his stomach, about Ann. He knew she was being held, or was dead. He knew he'd be through if she was dead. Never again, if he got out of this mess, would he work on a case with somebody he cared for terribly. What was it Delia Young had said? "I feel hollow inside." That was the way thinking about Ann made him feel.

Who could be holding her? He wondered if Williams was doing anything about her. He hadn't seen him all evening. He wondered what he would do when daylight came. He'd have to call in the police. Imagine a private detective asking help . . .

A scream, so brief he hardly believed his ears, sounded in the corridor. The sound was not repeated. What the hell? He found his revolver and slid out of the chair.

At the same instant the door to the room opened. Sudden draft made the muslin curtains dance wildly. A bulky woman with a floppy hat and a fur coat tiptoed toward the bed, a pillow in her hands. Crane said, "I've got you!" The woman dropped the pillow, fired two shots in his direction. The yellow flare of her gun blinded Crane. He crouched under the fluttering curtains and fired a shot at the door. His revolver made a deeper noise than the woman's. Acrid smoke stung his nose, his eyes. Together, making an enormous noise, he and the woman fired again.

"You bastard!" said the woman. Her voice was husky, like Delia Young's.

She let go one more shot, shattered the windowpane and fled. Crane ran to the door, stepped out into the corridor. The woman was three quarters of the way down the corridor in the direction of the elevator. She was running, and a blue skirt flared out under the brown fur coat. She was a big woman with muscular legs. Her hat hid the color of her hair.

Swinging down his revolver in a smooth arc, Crane took a careful shot at her. The revolver made a swell echo in the corridor. He didn't see that the shot had taken effect, though. Still running, the woman rounded the turn by the elevator.

Miss Edens was behind Crane.

"Who was it?"

"I don't know."

He started to run along the corridor. She ran after him, said:

"It sounds like the fall of Shanghai."

Their progress was abruptly halted by the woman. She leaned suddenly around the corner, took a pot shot at Crane. Floppy hat, coat collar, shielded her face. Miss Edens ducked into her anteroom. Crane, further along, leaped for the door to Room 417, opened it, backed into the room.

The woman fired another shot and Crane went further into the room. Behind him a woman began to scream.

"For God's sake, lady!" he said. "I won't hurt you."

He stuck his head out the door; the woman was gone. He stepped into the corridor. Nothing happened. He heard the whine of the elevator. He ran down the corridor, almost tripped over the body of a woman in a nurse's uniform. She was lying on the cement floor beside a table with a telephone on it, her head in a pool of blood. A chair had toppled across her feet.

The elevator was an automatic one. The golden arrow on the circle of Roman numerals above the glass doors was moving counterclockwise between III and II. Crane seized the phone.

"Hello. Hello! Goddamn it! Hello!" His thumb jiggled the hook. "Hello. Are there guards from March & Company in the lobby? . . . Well, tell 'em to stop whoever's coming down in the elevator. Quick!"

He dropped the receiver. Miss Edens was bending over the floor nurse.

"Is she dead?" he asked.

"I don't think so."

The golden arrow reached I, promptly started up again. Gray smoke swirled through the corridor. Miss Edens lifted the nurse's head, pushed a black leather chair pad under it. The nurse moaned softly. The golden arrow passed II.

Crane stared at it. "She's coming back."

Miss Edens said, "She's not!"

Crane looked at the .38. He had two shots. "Maybe she'll get off at three," he said.

The woman in 417 screamed. Her voice was shrill with terror; it made shivers run along Crane's spine. She screamed, caught her breath in a sob, screamed again.

The golden arrow went by III.

"You better get the hell out of here," Crane said to Miss Edens.

He pulled the reception desk from the wall, put a foot against one leg, with his free hand sent it to the floor on its side. Temperature charts zigzagged through the air; pencils, erasers, paper clips, chewing gum, a thermometer slid to the floor; the telephone smashed on the cement.

The woman in 417 screamed.

He slid the nurse's feet out of the way, knelt behind the table. She had on half-length silk hose, her thighs were bare. He could see a light behind the semiopaque glass doors of the shaft. He steadied his revolver hand on the upper edge of the table. Miss Edens was standing in a doorway farther up the corridor.

With a metallic click, the elevator reached IV. Crane crouched behind the table, aimed the revolver at the door. Squeeze the trigger, he kept thinking, squeeze the trigger. The nurse was conscious. She watched him through eyes bright with fear.

The elevator door slid open and Alice March stepped into the corridor, a sweet smile on her plump face, white flowers in her arms, a floppy hat on her head.

CHAPTER XIX

IN THE PORCELAIN-WALLED hospital canteen, Crane brooded over coffee liberally laced with whisky. He felt very bad. He blamed himself for the woman's escape; he still didn't know how to pin the crimes on the murderer; he felt he had failed Ann. He wished he wasn't a detective.

At his table, having coffee and hamburger sandwiches, was practically everyone in any way connected with the case. Dr Rutledge had returned after four hours' sleep, and the others were staying all night in the hospital, despite the fact that Simeon March had passed his crisis a few minutes after the shooting and had briefly regained consciousness.

Alice March was telling the others in her sweet, malicious voice how she felt when she was confronted with Crane's revolver.

"I really thought he'd run amuck," she said. "Especially when I saw the nurse lying in a pond of blood."

Peter March, his skin dead white under a blue growth of beard, listened to her with a bewildered air.

"I still don't understand all this," he said.

Between bites of hamburger, Dr Rutledge told the entire story from the time he had agreed to put Crane in Simeon March's room to the escape of the intruder. He talked mostly to Carmel, whose lovely face again reminded Crane of a tinted mask, aloof and serene, yet somehow watchful.

Further down the porcelain table was Dr Woodrin. His round face looked tired and some of the pink had faded. He listened to Dr Rutledge and drank black coffee.

"Crane thought the murderer might come back . . . " Dr Rutledge said.

Well, the plan *had* worked, Crane thought, drinking some of the coffee. Only he had muffed it. He supposed a braver man would have been closer behind the intruder, close enough to see her take the metal emergency stairs leading to the roof.

He'd just about got straight in his mind what had happened. The woman, after driving him into the room with the screaming lady, had run for the elevator, only to find someone (Alice March) had called it down. So she had ducked through a door marked Exit and had run up on the roof.

He'd been so dumfounded when Alice had walked out of the returning elevator, Crane admitted, that he hadn't thought of the possibility of another exit. He'd felt as if the woman had blown away like a puff of smoke. He'd just stared at Alice's astonished face.

A second later the guards from March & Company had arrived by way of the regular stairs, and he learned from them that Alice was already going up in the elevator when they reached it.

And it was Alice March who had finally said:

"Couldn't she have gone through that little door?"

On the metal stairs they had found traces of blood. A few drops had made . . . . on the steps, and there were two maroon smudges on the steel handrail.

"Must have winged her," one of the guards said.

"Not bad, though," the other said.

There had been a guard at the foot of the outside fire escape, and for a time Crane had hoped he might have caught the woman. But the trail of blood drops led two stories down the escape, then perilously crossed to an open window in the Nurses' Home adjoining City Hospital. Once in this building, the woman had walked down the back fire escape into the alley.

Crane took another drink of the spiked coffee. He had only himself to blame. Still he couldn't be expected to surround all the buildings in the neighborhood; he didn't have enough men, anyway. He . . .

Dr Rutledge had finished his story. Peter asked Crane, "Where's Ann?"

Crane said, "She's home, I think." He suddenly felt sick inside.

"What would she think if she knew you were mixed up in this shooting?" Carmel asked.

Her attitude toward the attack upon Simeon March, and the revelation that his being gassed in his garage was not an accident, Crane saw, was like the other Marchs, and Dr Woodrin too. They appeared to have known all the time something was wrong and were relieved it had finally been pointed out. But they still weren't discussing the matter.

He supposed he understood that, especially when the person you were discussing it with might be the murderer.

He answered Carmel's question. "She'd be surprised."

Alice asked, "Doesn't she know you've been acting as an amateur detective?"

Crane shook his head. He wished they wouldn't talk about Ann. He said, "Excuse me," and went to the telephone and called his house. His heart fluttered as the bell rang and rang. There was no answer. He wondered where Williams was.

They were talking about the floor nurse when he returned to the table.

"All that blood," Dr Rutledge was saying, "was a simple nosebleed. She's all right now."

Dr Woodrin said, "Too bad she didn't get a good look at the woman who hit her."

"She apparently creeps up behind her victims," Dr Rutledge said. "Simeon March didn't see her, either."

Mr March's brief account of the events in his garage, Crane admitted, had substantiated Williams' theory. The old man told them he was getting into his sedan when someone threw a blanket over his head. He struggled, but he was easily overpowered. He was thrown to the floor, tied, and someone started the engine in his sedan. Presently he began to breathe gas . . . and then he woke up in bed.

Crane's mind went back to Ann. Why had she disappeared? Was she a prisoner? Could she still be alive? Or was she dead of gas?

Carmel asked Dr Rutledge when Simeon March would be able to go home. The doctor said not for several days.

"We'll have to keep the guards here, then," Peter said.

Alice March said, "That woman will never come back now."

"I'm not taking any chances," Peter said.

Crane spoke to Dr Woodrin. "If the woman had smothered him with her pillow and escaped without anyone seeing her, would you have been able to tell what had happened?"

"It would 've been a perfect crime," Dr Woodrin said. "We'd have thought it was the gas."

The idea was pretty horrible. The murderer was smart! And ruthless! Crane felt a conviction that Ann had stumbled upon the truth and had been removed. Well, he'd spend the rest of his life . . .

Carmel asked him, "Would you like some more coffee and whisky?"

"I'd like some whisky."

She asked Dr Rutledge for his whisky and filled Crane's cup halfway up. "You look sick," she said.

"I am sick."

"It wasn't your fault the woman got away."

"I'd have caught her if I'd been braver."

"I think you were very brave."

"I was lousy."

"No."

A white-coated attendant tapped him on the shoulder. "You're wanted on the phone, Mr Crane."

It was Williams. He was very excited about something.

"I can't hear you," Crane said.

Williams' voice sounded as though he was trying to shout through a long section of pipe. "Damn it! I'm telling you I've got the dame spotted."

"What dame?"

"The dame who raised all the hell in the hospital."

Crane was silent and Williams said:

"Can't you hear me? *The dame who raised . . .*"

"I hear you, but I don't believe you," Crane said.

"But, Bill, I spotted her when she came down the fire escape back of the Nurses' Home. I saw the gun she had, so I followed her. She went . . ."

"Where are you?" Crane broke in excitedly.

"I don't know as I'll tell you, doubting me like that."

"Don't be coy," Crane said. "You're wonderful. You're a great detective. You're smarter than I am. I love you. Will you marry me? Will you tell me where the hell you are?"

"State highway 20—the first farmhouse to the right after the intersection of the Charlesville Pike."

"Anybody with her?"

"She went in alone, but the place may be loaded down."

"We'll be along in ten minutes."

"Like hell you will! It's twenty miles."

"Fifteen minutes then."

Williams was sitting on the running board of a rented coupé. His black eyes blinked at the array of automobiles.

"You call out the militia?"

Crane got out of Dr Woodrin's car. "Everybody insisted on coming."

Carmel March, with Peter in her convertible, called out excitedly, "Where to now?"

"Women, too?" Williams asked disgustedly.

"We couldn't keep 'em at home."

"There 'll be shooting."

"They'll stay back."

"Well, let's go."

Williams had them drive without lights a half mile down the cement road, then signaled for all the cars to stop. About one hundred yards ahead was a side road, a gray streak against the black countryside.

"We'll walk from here," he said.

Peter March told the women to wait with the cars. He left a guard to watch the side road. "Stop anybody who drives out," he said.

In the party were three more guards, Dr Woodrin, Dr Rutledge, Peter March, Williams and Crane.

While the others discussed plans for the attack, Crane took a flashlight, covered it with his coat so there would be no glow, examined the drive. He felt great excitement when he found a series of small craters on the soft earth. The treads were exactly like those made by the marksman's car at the Duck Club.

Dr Rutledge, coming over to him from the group, asked, "What are you doing?"

"I've found some fresh tire tracks."

They stood together while the whispered discussion continued. Crane asked the doctor, "Have you any methylene blue with you?"

"I think so. Why?"

"We might run into someone who has been gassed." He was thinking of Ann. "How long after would it work?"

"Depends upon how much gas they've had."

"How often do you give the injections?"

"That depends upon the patient."

"How often do you spray them?"

"You don't spray. Where 'd you get that idea?"

"I don't know. I thought somebody told me you did."

The plan had evidently been decided upon, because Williams touched Crane, said, "Let's go."

They started and Peter March, just ahead, whispered to Williams, "You're sure she's there?"

"I know she went in."

The road seemed to be descending. At the same time it began to wind. Clumps of trees, bushes, tall grass lined both sides. They had to halt now and then while the leaders felt out the way. It was very cold and still.

"How'd you follow her?" Peter March asked.

"She drove slow as hell, to keep from being stopped by cops, I guess," Williams said. "I was able to keep up with my lights off."

"I mean through this," Peter said.

"Oh. I didn't come in here. When she turned off I stopped and watched her headlights. I could see her drive down to a house and switch off the lights."

"And then you went to a farmhouse and telephoned?"

"Yeah."

They had got off the road again. One of the guards

lit a match. The orange flame showed trees, white faces; then someone knocked the match out of the guard's hand. "You fool!" Dr Woodrin said. "Want to give us away?"

Williams found the road. It wasn't completely dark, and Crane could see Peter's back, just ahead of him. The sky, above a tangle of half-bare branches, was mauve. It was only an hour to sunrise. Suddenly Williams halted.

"There's the house."

Directly ahead of them was a very faint rectangle of yellow light. For a moment it looked as though the light was floating high in the air, then they saw the gray outline of a two-story farmhouse. The rectangle was a window on the second floor.

"Somebody's up," Williams said.

Whispering, they decided to send four men around the house. The other four would try to get inside without attracting attention. At the sound of shooting, the four outside would rush the house.

Williams took it for granted he would be one of the four to go inside. Everybody took it for granted Crane would be another. Peter made it three. That left one more. Dr Rutledge said he'd go, but Crane objected.

"It's not your show," he said.

Dr Woodrin had been examining the house at a little distance from the group. He returned and said, "I'm going. John and Richard . . . Talmadge . . . They were my best friends. It's certainly *my* show."

Chapter XX

A cautious examination of the farmhouse disclosed locked windows and doors. The color of the night was Oxford gray; in the sky only the big stars remained. There was no wind. Williams led them to the front door, tried a master key in the lock. After a moment it turned and they followed him inside.

The hall had a musty smell, like that of a room shut up for a long time. There was a smell of dry leather, of dust, of mildewed fabric, of mice, of rotting wood. The air felt moist and warm on their faces.

Under their feet, the floor creaked faintly. They halted, holding their breaths.

There was talking upstairs. The voices were muffled; it was impossible to tell if the speakers were men or women. The conversation was leisurely; a rumble of words, a long silence, a murmured reply.

A rod of light extended from Williams' fountain-pen flashlight to a green rug, so worn that cross threads of the fabric showed through the nap. Further ahead were stairs and a ten-foot landing. On the left the oak balustrade had been partially torn loose from the stairs. It tilted crazily, like a section of railroad track uprooted by flood. Over the landing a tattered piece of muslin partially cloaked a square window.

Williams touched Crane's arm. They started up the stairs, keeping close to the wall on the right. On the landing Crane was surprised to see that the square window was made up of small, colored panes; green, red, blue, orange and brown. The next flight of stairs looked safer.

A cold draft flowed along the second-floor hall, numbed their wrists and ankles. The voices were louder now, but it was not possible to distinguish the words. Light stained the hall floor through a crack under a door fifteen feet to the right.

Suddenly a man laughed hoarsely. Crane nearly lost his balance; his startled jerk carried him against the wall; he put up his left hand to save himself. Cobwebs stuck to his fingers. He realized the man was laughing in the room with the light. He tried to scrape the cobwebs off his hand with the barrel of his revolver. He was scared as hell.

They went along the hall to the door. A woman was

laughing with the man; both sounded a little drunk. The man, between laughs, said in a deep voice:

"Like a boilerworks, by golly!"

He pounded a table with his fist, then they both laughed.

Williams' mouth was against Crane's right ear. "The doc hasn't got a gun. He'll bust the door with his shoulders, bust in, and you and Peter and me'll cover..."

Vicious snarls, loud barking broke out somewhere in back of the house. A pistol went off twice. Crane could see the flashes through the colored window. The dog yelped once and was silent.

Dr Woodrin said, "Come on." He hit the door with his shoulder; it gave with a crack like a big firecracker. He staggered into the room. Crane, beside Williams and a step ahead of Peter March, followed.

Two flickering oil lamps on a bare table threw jaundiced light over half the room. They held in uncertain rays a carrot-haired woman in a gaudy cotton wrapper; a quart of rye whisky and two partially filled glasses; a mussed bed on which sat a man wearing a blue skirt and an underwear top. The woman was Delia Young. She was seated on a chair across the table from the bed; her painted face was turned in the direction of the shots. The man was looking that way, too, but his face was in shadow. There was a shapeless bundle of clothes in a corner of the room. A tight bandage circled the man's left arm just above the elbow.

It seemed, to Crane, the action was like that in a prizefight motion picture which has been halted for an instant to let the audience see a particular punch. The crack of the door was the signal for the halt; their arrival in the room started the reel again.

Delia Young screamed. The man bent over and fumbled among the bedcovers. Dr Woodrin's voice shook the windows.

"We've got you this time."

Delia Young screamed. The bundle of clothes in the corner moved. The man's hand came around in a swift arc. A sliced second before his pistol went off, Dr Woodrin, almost between Crane and the man, dropped on the floor. Like an echo, Williams' revolver answered the pistol. Crane fired at the man, too. They both fired again. "You . . . you . . . " the man muttered. His body suddenly flabby, he pitched forward on the floor. Delia Young screamed again.

"Pipe down, tutz," Williams said.

Crane moved a step forward, his smoking revolver still pointed at the bed. Dr Woodrin got off the floor. Crane looked down at the body. It was Slats Donovan and he was dead. Peter March hurried to the bundle in the corner. Crane lifted the bottle of rye from the table. It was half full. He wiped the neck with the palm of his hand, took a long drink.

"My God!" he said when he finished. "Oh, my God!"

Delia Young stopped screaming. Her eyes were frightened behind smears of blue mascara. Williams put his hands under Donovan's armpits.

"Give me a hand, Bill."

They put the body on the bed. Crane discovered blood on his left hand, his left wrist. He couldn't find a handkerchief in the pockets on his right side and he didn't want to spoil his clothes by searching with the left hand. He opened his coat, wiped the hand on his shirt. It was only a two-dollar shirt.

Peter March was lifting the bundle in the corner. It was Ann Fortune, and she had been bound and gagged. Crane felt a great relief. He wondered how she had found the house. She was smiling at Peter.

Crane said, "Lucky for you, baby, we came along."

Ann smiled at him. "Hello, Bill," she said. Her hair was the color of the straw that champagne bottles come in. "I'd almost given you up." Her green eyes went back to Peter. "Thanks for untying me," she said to him.

That's gratitude for you, Crane thought. You risk your life saving a gal, and who does she thank? The other guy!

Williams said disgustedly, "All this work chasing after clues, and it turns out to be a plain gangster job."

Dr Woodrin was looking at Donovan. "That was a close one." There was no pink in his face.

Williams said, "It took guts to do what you did without a gun." He stared at Dr Woodrin's white face. "He didn't wing you, did he?"

"No."

"Where'd his shot go?"

Nobody knew, and Williams added, "Good thing Bill and I were quick."

Delia Young was watching them. "Damn you all for a bunch of murderers," she said in her husky voice.

Dr Rutledge and the guards had come upstairs and goggled at the body and Delia Young. Williams was describing the shooting when Carmel and Alice March arrived in two of the cars.

"We just *had* to know what happened," Alice said.

Carmel's dark eyes were on Ann, beside Peter. "How in the world did you get here?" she asked.

Ann said, "I thought Slats Donovan was the murderer. So I found out where Delia Young was through a girl at the Crimson Cat, but Donovan surprised me trying to get into the house."

Carmel said, "Slats Donovan killed John and Richard?"

"And Talmadge." Peter March looked at Ann. "It was clever of you to figure that out."

"Just a lousy gangster job," Williams said.

Ann said, "It wasn't so clever to get caught."

"But what happened here?" Alice March persisted.

Peter repeated the story of the shooting to Carmel and Alice.

"I'm glad you're safe," Crane said to Ann.

"You didn't show it." Her voice was cool. "Letting somebody else untie me."

Crane shrugged his shoulders. He sat on the table and crooked a finger at Williams.

"Get Doctor Woodrin's medicine bag for me," he said in a low voice. "One of the gals brought his car down."

"Hell!" Williams said. "Donovan's dead."

"I want it."

Williams' black eyes were suddenly alarmed. "He didn't wing you, did he, Bill?"

Crane smiled at him. "Get the bag."

Peter March was still talking. "You really ought to

thank me for saving you," Crane said to Ann. "Me and Doc Williams. I couldn't untie you because I was too busy with Donovan."

"That was close," she admitted. "I don't see how his shot missed you."

Crane saw Williams in the hall. He went out and took the bag from him, opened it, fumbled among its contents.

"What're you looking for?" Williams asked. "A drink?"

Someone in the room called, "Crane!"

There were a number of medical articles in his hand: a silver thermometer case, a steel probe, some cotton, an atomizer, a glass bottle of capsules. He carried these back into the room.

Peter March asked, "Any reason we can't cart away the body?"

"I don't know of any."

"What'll we do with the woman?"

"Let her go," Ann said. "She was practically a prisoner."

Alice March was standing with Dr Rutledge. "I don't understand why Donovan killed Richard . . . and and everybody." Her plump face was bewildered.

Williams jerked a thumb toward the bed. "Why don't you ask him?"

Peter March said, "He hated the whole March family because March & Company fired him."

Crane put the medical objects on the table beside the bottle of rye. He didn't feel so good. He took a drink, sat on the table, put the bottle down. He sat with his back arched, his stomach pulled in.

Ann was watching him. "Are you all right, Bill?"

He smiled at her. "Sure." He wished he didn't like her so much. He picked up the atomizer, pointed it at his nose, gave the rubber bulb a tentative squeeze. He sneezed.

Dr Rutledge said to Peter March, "There must have been more of a motive than revenge."

Crane put the atomizer on the table, began to clean his nails with the steel probe. "There was," he said.

"What was it?" Peter March asked.

Crane ignored him. He put the probe down, took his revolver from his pocket. He gave it to Williams.

"Don't let Doctor Woodrin leave the room," he said.

There was silence as Williams aimed the revolver at the physician.

Then Dr Woodrin said, "What's the big idea?" His pink-and-white face was angry. "If you're playing a joke, I don't . . ."

"Save it," Williams said.

"Drop him if he moves," Crane said.

Carmel March exclaimed, "You must be mad."

"Am I?" Crane took the atomizer, squirted it at her. "With this I purify you." He gave the rubber bulb a couple of squeezes. He felt a little light headed.

They certainly thought he had gone crazy. Even Williams was a little dubious. He thought, maybe he's just drunk. He wondered if the rye was doped.

The fine spray from the atomizer fogged Carmel's head, beaded on her mink coat, floated past Peter March.

"Perfume!" he said.

Carmel cried, "My gardenia!"

Crane gave the atomizer a final squeeze. "Would a corpse by any other name smell so sweet?" he inquired, and turned to Peter March. "Can you search the doctor's car?"

Peter March nodded to a guard by the door.

Crane spoke to Dr Woodrin. "Clever idea, wasn't it, to try to implicate Carmel?"

"You're insane," Dr Woodrin said.

Dr Rutledge said, "I know I am. For God's sake, Crane, tell us what it's all about."

Crane felt very tired. The rye didn't seem to do much good, but he took another drink.

"It's about perfume, oily water, a plagiarist and duck shooting," he said.

Carmel March gasped. "Duck shooting?"

"Well, the Duck Club then. They've found oil in Michigan, near Lansing, and in Illinois." Crane spoke to Peter March. "But there's probably a hell of a lot more right under your great-grandfather's land."

Even the guards gaped at him. He went on: "Woodrin knows this. Having been an oil-company doctor, he'd be bound to know a lot about oil. Oil seepage; the geologic formation of the duck grounds tipped him off, but he couldn't buy the property."

The guard who was searching Dr Woodrin's car appeared with a Scotch-plaid blanket and a tennis net. "They were in the rumble," he said, going away again.

Crane continued, "There was little danger of the oil being discovered since the Marchs aren't oil people, even though oil seepage killed fish in the pools, and there are no wells within five hundred miles to make them think of oil. But as a trustee of the great-grandfather's estate, Woodrin could sell the land to himself . . . *once the last March had died.*"

His face incredulous, Peter March stared at the doctor. "All those murders to get possession of an oil field?"

"Oh, he hated all of you, too."

Carmel gasped, "Hated us?"

"Sure. You were rich; he wasn't. When he had a chance to make money, with Donovan and Talmadge, in the night-club business, John spoiled it. So he went after the oil. How much is an oil field worth? A million dollars? Fifty million?"

Williams said, "Some guys 'll murder for fifty bucks."

Dr Woodrin's round face was the color of caramel ice cream. "Do you believe all this nonsense?" he demanded of Peter.

Crane put an elbow on his thigh, leaned his chin on his palm. He was more comfortable doubled over, but he felt lousy. He said, "Now for the murders, in the order . . ."

The guard interrupted him by tossing coils of white rubber hose on the floor. "That's all," he said.

"Swell!" said Crane, looking at the hose. "There's the real proof."

Williams' revolver went off with a tremendous boom. It seemed as though the noise had caused Dr Woodrin to make a startled leap for the door, but it must have followed the leap because the bullet caught him just as he entered the hall. He took two heavy steps forward, crashed headlong down the stairs.

Alice March screamed, but Carmel silenced her, saying, "Shut up, you fat fool!"

Crane said, "Nice shot, Williams."

Led by Dr Rutledge, everyone but Ann and Delia Young went out into the hall. Delia Young sat motionless in her chair. Crane remained on the table and had another drink. He drank bent over. He wondered if Ann was angry because he was drinking.

"Aren't you going to thank me for saving you?" he asked her.

Ann said, "And it wasn't Donovan after all?" Her green eyes were round.

"I really think you ought to thank me," Crane said.

The bullet had penetrated the hip of Dr Woodrin. It was a flesh wound and there was a lot of blood. Carmel helped Dr Rutledge with bandages, and then two guards were told to take Woodrin to City Hospital. "Notify the police," Peter March said. "We'll be right in."

Crane said to those at the top of the stairs, "You better let me finish before I fall over."

They came back into the room.

"The idea was to make all the murders look like accidents and a suicide," he went on. "When Richard passed out in his car at the Country Club the doctor simply attached the hose to the exhaust pipe, ran it through a window, waited until he was dead, then took away the hose. Richard was drunk and couldn't smell the gas."

Dr Rutledge said, "It's practically odorless anyway."

"John's death was a little more difficult. Woodrin met him in his garage, threw the Scotch blanket over his head, muffling his shouts, and then wound him up in the tennis net. (You remember he always carried a tennis net with him?) That was to hold him without bruising his body. Then the carbon monoxide was hosed under the blanket."

"That's ghastly!" Carmel exclaimed.

With a splutter, Dr Woodrin's car started, went off in low gear. A small wind had come up with the dawn, was making the shades rustle. Away from the house, the car went into second.

"Talmadge died like Richard, in his own car."

Williams asked, "But why wasn't he in the driver's seat?"

"That showed he'd been tricked. Woodrin, on some pretext, arranged to meet Talmadge outside during the dance. The doctor went out early, rigged up the hose in Talmadge's car, then started the motor, ostensibly to allow the heater to warm the inside of the sedan. When Talmadge arrived, Woodrin was in the driver's seat, carefully breathing through a crack in the door, and the car was full of monoxide."

Carmel cried, "But why didn't Talmadge smell the gas?"

"It's nearly odorless, as Dr Rutledge just said . . . and he had a bad cold."

"Woodrin couldn't breathe through the crack after Talmadge was there," Peter objected. "That would be too obvious. Why wasn't he overcome, too?"

"He stayed only a moment or two," said Crane. "Then he framed an excuse to leave him, for a letter, or to get someone. For anything. He closed the door behind him. It was a cold night; the heat felt good, even though Talmadge was probably nervous about carbon monoxide, but there was also a psychological reason why the motor wasn't turned off."

There was a moment of silence.

"The reason was politeness. Woodrin had started the engine and the heater because he was cold; it would be impolite of Talmadge to turn it off, even though it was his car. So he died while Woodrin watched from a safe distance, was dead when Woodrin came back to remove the hose."

Peter March asked, "But why the note in John's case, when the deaths passed as accidents?"

"Woodrin didn't want an investigation. He forged the note so your family, if suspicion arose, would stop their investigation when they discovered John killed Richard, then himself. And to block a police investigation, he helped Carmel set the stage with tools on the garage floor and the hood of the sedan raised . . . so the coroner's jury would call the death accidental."

"Wasn't the forged note a big risk?" Dr Rutledge asked.

"No." Crane had difficulty keeping his eyes open. "In the excitement of the discovery, Carmel wouldn't study it. And it was promptly destroyed."

Behind the house a rooster crowed. The two oil lamps threw hardly any light. Ann was watching Crane.

Crane sighed and took another drink. He hoped that solved everything. He felt awful; even the drink didn't help.

Peter said, "But what about Dad? Woodrin was with us when the attempt was made on him."

"That was Donovan, accomplishing a little plagiarism on what he'd learned of the murders from me and from Delia Young. He'd always hated Simeon March, and when he learned how people could be killed with carbon

monoxide, he thought he'd muscle in on the murders."
Crane crossed his arms over his stomach. "Only he
bungled the job. *He forgot the gardenia.* That's how I
knew it wasn't the real murderer."

Peter asked, "Do you suppose he knew Woodrin was
doing the murders?"

"I think so. I wouldn't be surprised if he saw Woodrin
fix Talmadge's car; he was at the Country Club that
night."

Dr Rutledge said, "And when Mr March didn't die,
Donovan was afraid he'd been identified, so he had to
try again."

Crane nodded.

"How did you happen to suspect Woodrin?" Alice
March asked.

"His surprise when Simeon March was gassed. He'd
taken the other deaths so calmly. He just couldn't
believe it. Then the atomizer when he came into the
hospital room to treat Mr March. You don't use an
atomizer to treat carbon monoxide poisoning."

Dr Rutledge asked, "You think he was going to
smother Mr March, then spray the gardenia around?"

"I'm sure of it." Crane closed his eyes for a second.
"And the clinching clue was the oily water at the Duck
Club."

"Who fired the shots at the Duck Club?" Peter asked.

"Donovan. He attacked Simeon March, then came out there. He wanted to frighten me; he was afraid I knew too much."

Peter asked, "How did you figure out the use of the net and the hose?"

"I guessed at the net, and smelled rubber on the exhaust pipe."

Delia Young, still sitting in the chair, said huskily, "I thought you was a dick, Arthur."

Peter was nodding his head. "And Woodrin was eager to be in the death here, to make sure Donovan was killed before he could produce alibis for John's and Richard's deaths."

Crane said, "It took guts to take the chance of dodging Slats' bullets until we killed him, but he was desperate. And he didn't dare shoot Slats himself; he knew that would throw suspicion on him."

Williams said, "Slats damn near got him, too."

Crane said, "And that brings down the curtain."

He poured himself another drink, was surprised to see the bottle was nearly empty. Dr Rutledge and the remaining guard led the way down the stairs. Ann watched Peter and Carmel leave the room. Williams went by with Delia Young. He winked at Crane. Alice March called to Carmel and Peter, "Wait for me." She was the last to leave, brushing past Ann at the door. Crane closed his eyes, opened them and saw Ann still there, closed them again.

After a long time she asked, "Are you sick, Bill?"

"No."

"You look awfully pale."

He let his head drop against one shoulder. "I'm all right."

Her voice was alarmed. "Bill!" She came to the table. "What's the matter?"

"Nothing."

"You're not hurt?"

"Not very much."

She clutched his arm. "Where?"

He uttered a cry of pain. "Don't touch me." He sat upright with a tremendous effort. "Please go away." He pressed both hands against his chest. "Please."

"Bill!" She pulled his hands away, opened his coat. "You've been shot! There's blood all over your shirt!"

"I'm all right."

"But, Bill, why didn't you have the doctors . . . " Her green eyes widened. "Is it as bad as that?"

He nodded slowly.

"Oh, darling, don't die! I couldn't bear to have you die." She looked at him. "Isn't there anything . . . ?"

"You can . . . thank me . . . for saving you."

"Of course I thank you, Bill." Her hands opened the bloody shirt. "I was only angry because you let Peter . . . " She searched in vain for the wound. She let go of the shirt, looked up at his face.

"You louse!" she said. "Fooling me like that! I'll never speak to you again as long as I live."

"Darling," he said, grinning, "then you'll make me an ideal wife."

There is an extensive list of NO EXIT PRESS crime titles to choose from. All the books can be obtained from Oldcastle Books Ltd, 18 Coleswood Road, Harpenden, Herts AL5 1EQ by sending a cheque/P.O. (or quoting your credit card number and expiry date) for the appropriate amount + 10% as a contribution to Postage & Packing.

Alternatively, you can send for FREE details of the NO EXIT PRESS CRIME BOOK CLUB, which includes many special offers on NO EXIT PRESS titles and full information on forthcoming books. Please write clearly stating your full name and address.

NO EXIT PRESS Vintage Crime

Classic crime novels by the contemporaries of Chandler & Hammett that typify the hard-boiled heyday of American crime fiction.

FAST ONE — Paul Cain £3.95pb, £9.95hb

Possibly the toughest, tough-guy story ever written. Set in depression Los Angeles, it has a surreal quality that is positively hypnotic. It is the saga of gunman-gambler Gerry Kells and his dipsomaniacal lover, S Granquist (she has no first name), who rearrange the L.A. underworld and disappear in an explosive climax that matches their first appearance. The pace is incredible and the complex plot, with its twists and turns, defies summary.

SEVEN SLAYERS — Paul Cain £3.99pb, £9.95hb

A superb collection of seven stories about seven star crossed killers and the sole follow up to the very successful Fast One. Peopled by racketeers, con men, dope pushers, private detectives, cops, newspapermen and women of some virtue or none at all. Seven Slayers is as intense a 'noir' portrait of depression era America as those painted by Horace McCoy and James M Cain.

THE DEAD DON'T CARE — Jonathan Latimer £3.95pb, £9.95hb

Meet Bill Crane, the hard-boiled P.I., and his two sidekicks, O'Malley and Doc Williams. The locale of the cyclonic action is a large Florida estate near Miami. A varied cast includes a former tragic actress turned dipso, a gigolo, a 'Babe' from Minsky's, a broken down welterweight and an exotic Mayan dancer. Kidnapping and murder give the final shake to the cocktail and provide an explosive and shocking climax.

THE LADY IN THE MORGUE — Jonathan Latimer £3.99pb, £9.95hb

Crime was on the up. People sang of Ding-Dong Daddy, skirts were long and lives were short, violin cases mostly sported machine guns. Bill Crane thought it was a pretty wonderful time. He was in the Chicago morgue at the height of summer, trying to cool off and learn the identity of its most beautiful inmate. So-called Alice Ross had been found hanging, absolutely naked, in the room of a honky tonk hotel. His orders were to find out who she really was. Alice was stolen from her slab that night! Thus began the crazy hunt for a body and a name, through lousy hotels, dancehalls and penthouses, with occasional side trips to bed to bar to blonde and back again.

MURDER IN THE MADHOUSE — Jonathan Latimer £3.99pb, £9.95hb

Hard drinking, hard living Bill Crane in his first case has himself committed incognito to a private sanitarium for the mentally insane to protect rich, little Ms Van Camp. Terror, violence and sudden death follow when a patient is found strangled with a bathrobe cord. The murderer strikes again but makes a fatal error in killing pleasant little mute, Mr Penny. The local police doubt Crane is a bonafide detective and believe he is suffering from delusions, the non-alcoholic kind. Despite all this, Crane breaks the case in a final scene of real dramatic fury.

HEADED FOR A HEARSE — Jonathan Latimer £3.99pb, £9.95hb

Death row, Chicago county jail. Robert Westland, convicted of his wife's murder, is six days from the 'chair'. What seems an iron clad case against Westland begins to fall apart as Bill Crane races against time to investigate the background of the major players and prove Westland's innocence. Westland's two brokerage partners; his hard drinking, hard riding cousin; enigmatic and exotic Ms Brentino; the amiable Ms Hogan; a secretive clerk; a tight-lipped valet and a dipso widow all have plenty to explain. Aided by a lime squeezer, a quart of whisky, a monkey wrench, a taxi cab, a stop watch and a deep sea diver, Crane cracks the case in this locked room classic.

GREEN ICE — Raoul Whitfield £3.99pb, £9.95hb
Watch out for Mal Ourney: where Mal goes, murder follows. It is on his heels as he walks out of Sing Sing after taking a man-slaughter rap for a dubious dame and follows him all the way on the trail of some sizzling hot emeralds — 'Green Ice'. "naked action pounded into tough compactness by staccato, hammer-like writing" Dashiell Hammett.

DEATH IN A BOWL — Raoul Whitfield £3.99pb, £9.95hb
Maestro Hans Reiner is on the podium, taking the fiddle players through a big crescendo. Then something goes off with a bang and it isn't the tympani! Reiner finds himself with a load of lead in the back — and a new tune: The Funeral March.

THE VIRGIN KILLS — Raoul Whitfield £3.99pb, £9.95hb
Millionaire gambler Eric Vennel's yacht sets sail for the regatta at Poughkeepsie with an oddball assortment of uneasy companions: Hardheaded sportswriter Al Conners; beautiful Hollywood ham, Carla Sard; Sard's nemesis tart-tongued scribbler Rita Veld; big ugly out of place bruiser Mick O'Rourke, and a glittering cross-section of east and west coast society. Rumours of Vennel's heavy betting on the regatta and a midnight attack by a masked intruder raise the tension . . . to the point of murder!

HALO IN BLOOD — Howard Browne £3.99pb, £9.95hb
Meet Paul Pine, Chicago P.I. Three seemingly unrelated events — the funeral of a pauper at which 12 clergymen from different faiths are the only mourners; Pine being hired by John Sandmark to dig up some dirt on the man intending to marry his daughter, Leona; and a run-in with the gangster, D'Allemand, where Pine is nearly killed delivering a $25,000 ransom in counterfeit bills — are woven into a complex and web of events that produces some explosive twists to the finale.

HALO FOR SATAN — Howard Browne £3.99pb, £9.95hb.

Raymond Wirtz has something everyone wants! His grace, the Bishop of Chicago; Lola North, "a girl who could turn out to be as pure as an easter lily or steeped in sin and fail to surprise you either way"; Louis Antuni, Chicago Godfather; Constance Benbrook, who "wasn't the type to curl up with anything as inanimate as a novel" and mysterious super criminal, Jafar Baijan — all want what Wirtz has . . . the ultimate religious artefact. Private Eye, Paul Pine is right in the middle. In the middle of a deadly obstacle race strewn with corpses, cops and beautiful women.

NO EXIT PRESS Contemporary Crime

A companion to Vintage Crime in the popular pocket book format that highlights both the classic and exciting new books from the past twenty years of American Crime Fiction. Contemporary Crime will feature in 1989 such titles as Day of the Ram by William Campbell Gault, Ask the Right Question by Michael Z Lewin, Act of Fear by Michael Collins, Dead Ringer and Castles Burning by Arthur Lyons all costing just £2.99.

HARD TRADE — Arthur Lyons £2.99pb

LA's most renowned detective, Jacob Asch is on the street once more in a startling tale of Californian political corruption. A troubled woman hires Asch to uncover the truth about the man she is to marry. When Asch discovers the man is gay and the woman is run down on her way to a hastily called meeting with Asch, it becomes clear something big is at stake. Serious money real estate schemes, the seamy side of LA gay life and a murder frame involve Asch in a major political scandal that costs him his licence and nearly his life.

THE KILLING FLOOR — Arthur Lyons £2.99pb

David Fein, owner of Supreme Packing, a slaughterhouse in a grimy little Californian town had a problem . . . he was a compulsive gambler. First he couldn't cover his losses from the takings so he got a loan and went into debt. By the time he took in Tortorello, a clean cut Harvard type but with 'Family' connections he was in big trouble. Now he had been missing for 4 days and his wife was frantic. Jake Bloom, old family friend puts her in touch with Jacob Asch, who figures Fein is on a bender or in the sack with another woman — he's heard and seen it all before. But that's before he finds a body on the killing floor.

NO EXIT PRESS Contemporary Crime